GW01143837

A BALLET OF WASPS

And other works

Jonathan Bowden

TSTC

First Edition
Published December 2008

Printed in Great Britain

Cover design and layout by Daniel Smalley
Cover painting 'Anarch Bee-Man' by Jonathan Bowden

ISBN 978-0-9557402-6-8

TSTC

The Spinning Top Club
BM Refine
London
WC1N 3XX

www.jonathanbowden.co.uk

Study for Three Figures at the base of a Crucifixion
by Francis Bacon (1947)

Out they stand in orange
screaming like blinded bats
wrapped around in lintel
a mother's angel sings:
better were it, indeed, not to be born!

Dedicated to Dorothy Bowden (1931-1978)

Jonathan Bowden
Photo by Andrea Lioy

CONTENTS

A BALLET OF WASPS

a short story

ONE

Have you ever perused Sir James Frazer's *The Golden Bough*? Well, this is a tale which escaped from its twelve compendious volumes and extensive foot-notes...

TWO

A Woodsman bragged before a coterie of his drinking companions in eighteenth century White Russia. A large oaken table – with cross beams – lay in front of his gnarled hand. He grasped it using main force; while the other mitten contained within it a tankard of steaming ale. Who is not to say that it had been brewed from rare berries, or cast into a vat with variously exotic fruits like pomegranates? Do you hear? The Woodsman himself was stocky, oafish, slightly ill-kempt, and he happened to be wearing a fur-lined jacket made of boar skin. It glistened under the available lights… all of which kept up a subterranean glow from niches and corners. Each lamp, moreover, had tassels around it – and came attached to basalt pillars that dotted a cavernous inn. Perhaps it resembled the atmosphere of a converted barn; or alternatively, one of those pseudo-Transylvanian films which litter a Hammer House of Horror. Anyway, a rare trellis-work – appearing to be Tudor in origin – festooned the inner walls of this structure, rising up in its multiplicity from the ground. Ever more complicated Arabesques were then noticed, each one lifting up, tier on tier, so that they filled the inner canvas of these walls with straight black lines. In their complexity and allure, they seemed to notify one of Wyndham Lewis' military compositions from prior to the Great War. They virtually called out to you – in the manner of a board like *Planners* (*Happy Day*), dating from 1913. In it, a Front moves in a labile construction towards an unknown goal – each one blocked out by arrows. The picture transfigures its own Essence, if only by dint of oblivion… or necessarily, in a way which configures the Vienna Group painting of Ernst Fuchs. Might it encode a military architecture *a la* von Clausewitz, or more properly the demography of a new oblivion? Perhaps, in such a tracery, we can detect the dissident cartography of Guy Debord… or not?

THREE

Regardless of any of this, such biceps – that maximise a new skeleton's limbs – pass up the wall with the tracery of multiple spiders' webs. They denote the inner workings or tendons of the spine – after a fashion which accords with anatomical fissures. Possibly the cadavers of Professor Gunter von Hagens, as delineated in psychic paint, come into the frame here. Do you sense this eventuality, pathologically speaking? Although another option may become available – one that has to do with the architectonics of the hive, seeking succour, thereby, from Count Maurice de Maeterlinck's *The Life of Bees*… In a situation where insect colonisation is seen afresh, pursuant to those amazing cities which such creatures build in crevices or under the ground. Aren't all of these illustrations of Mega-city One achieved through entomology's ferment? Furthermore, at the heart of any *Drosophila's* drama or *Lepidoptera's* coldspring, we can acknowledge an occult art: even the Albigensian idealism that fired le Corbusier's modernism. Would it be useful to consult Ernst Junger's *The Glass Bees* now? May such caracoles bring forth a wasps' ballet?

FOUR

All the time our Woodsman's been hectoring his audience – another entity listened with growing impatience. Truly, no-one could put up with an indifferent shrug of the shoulders roundabouts! Especially since this night's wraith happened to be a Vampire. Such a Slavic type, racially speaking, sat hunched over in the corner of our travellers' rest. A relatively icy penumbra surrounded him, but more of the spirit than aught else. His eyes were dark and glowed in the face like coals; while 'its' hair came thick, straight and black upon the scalp. He continued to trespass a look of hunger all the way down to his pointy beard: after the fashion of a saturnine George V! Similarly, his skin-tone, chameleon like, waxed now yellow and then white under the lights… Whereupon, in dress' terms, he had about him a heavy grey mackintosh; a vessel or instrument of wrath, (this), which swept down to his knees. He denied the facility of a cape, but somehow came to seamlessly embody it. Yes, that's right: and at his throat our example of Anne Rice's Undead wore a cravat. Bright red or scarlet it was: with more than a hint about it of unobliging haemoglobin. His name didn't really suffice anymore. Some dared to whisper about the nomenclature of Lord Weirdorf (or Temple Bickerstaff) behind the webbing of each glove… Yet nothing came of it. For these purposes a tale like this – drawn from Russian folklore – doesn't have to provide nemesis with a name.

FIVE

To one side of our braggart sat a range of hearty spectators. They deliberated pipe in hand or open-mouthed, especially when confronted with tales of derring-do. Boisterous announcements of valour poured from the Woodsman's lips… While – in front of his rather helpless admirers – a litany of bottles, vodka glasses, fake liqueurs and malts littered a wooden bench. Immediately adjacent to and behind his hearers, however, a spear with a fluted end – plus a halberd or axe – found themselves attached to a wall bracket. The vampire listened on with greater peevishness… and became more & more aggrieved.

SIX

Eventually, the Woodsman staggered from the tavern, thence passing out into desolate conditions of ice and snow. He almost slipped on a treacherous strip of Jack Frost's bounty or loss… and this was before the Vampire pounced on him. His talons and teeth were exposed, and the two of them crashed down into barren wastes. It would be wrong to say that the forester put up no resistance, but the Undead's sinews stretched in an iron-hard way. No mortal man could hold out against such odds, at least in terms of the force with which the Woodsman was hurled to the glacier. Both his hands came up in order to ward off Bela Lugosi's charge… yet our man-bat proved too resourceful, sinister, approximate and empowered to provide contemporary resistance to. Once our gombeen man, convicted of his braggadocio, lay prone on the tundra… the Vampire leant across him with a daemonic mien. He seemed to lie aslant the other's body, licking his lips, and immediately he ripped out his heart and ate it! There occurred sudden convulsions in the Woodsman, even though these soon passed only to be substituted by stillness. Our Dracula's Guest then went even farther. Because, with a sharp or taloned finger, he opened up the belly of a passing rabbit. This he magically introduced into a cavity in the Woodsman's chest – before sealing it up again. Is one aware of the fact that an Undead's touch, witnessed at certain hours, might lead to defeat or a withdrawal of circumstances? With a clap of his hands the blood, gore, rents in one's clothing and so forth, all cleared away under a spectral or gibbous moon. *Avaunt thee*, it wasn't long after that all trace of a bat-hominid vanished, leaving our Woodsman prone on hardened slush. He came to surrounded by arctic conditions roundabout.

SEVEN

Afterwards, and to the surprise of many, our Woodsman made a miraculous recovery. Yet, in one respect, he was subtly and ineradicably changed. This must have to do with his capacity for courage. Since now, when late at night (and under an opalescent moon) he heard a wolf-hound howl, our man quaked with fear. Moreover, he often cringed anew, rolled himself into a ball and shrunk from the slightest sound, even foot-steps in the snow. Surely, the steppes answer to Sheridan le Fanu has inflicted a crushing blow or reverse? For the Woodsman's prize asset, his valour, had been taken from him. Might we draw a lesson from Aesop's fables here? Perhaps this story's moral is as follows:

bravery remains our highest virtue, but be careful where thou speakest of it!

FINIS

GOLGOTHA'S CENTURION

a story

PART THE FIRST

A hot day of Sicilian sunshine has ended; or fallen in balmy eventide over the town. Initially, the solar orb had been brutal in its heat, but now the hamlet's white-wash glowed with a refulgent cooling. Yes, the swash of sky behind seems to be streaked *avec* orange, green and turquoise. While those buildings which characterised a Sicilian hamlet – other than the ones made out of lava – appeared to be higgledy-piggledy or ramshackle in a golden haze. A few peasants were abroad – either walking about, mopping their brows, or knocking out the contents of clay pipes on various outposts. Most assuredly, since in the background and under a sky of brilliant azure, there lay a domed church with its spire scratching the surface of the heavens. Didn't it resemble one of those delicately classical or early Renaissance piles that contains the odd fresco, and which doubles pink or yellow in the light? Occasionally, a slight tincture of blue sweeps across a given department of wall. In the distance – and with a dramatic mountain rearing as a backdrop – a solitary figure hoves to. He is a man alone. He walks towards his village with a sureness of tread.

PART THE SECOND

The man concerned came of middle-size – with slacks on his legs and a faint velvet waistcoat flung across his torso. A hidden/panther-like power or suppression was observable in the limbs. He walked with a casual gait, but there had to be an undertone of menace to his stalk. His name, you ask? Frederico Borghese Gaati… remember it.

"It is him, HIM…", the old crone almost screeched in her husband's ear. In remarking this, Simone, an octogenarian dressed all in black recalled to mind a sibyl's presence… but not the one articulated by Michelangelo. "You see, eh? EH? He has returned, the brother of the whore… the scarlet woman, the one whom men mount in an ecstasy of forgiveness." As she lisped these words, perchance, could one detect a certain nostalgia or disappointment in her voice? "Hush woman, mask those entreaties with silence", commanded her husband. He was an old man, possibly five or six years younger than his spouse, whose face abbreviated some dimpled suet. This elderly member of the chorus stood erect, clay pipe in hand, and looked vaguely like a sentinel or a watchman… as Gaati slouched past. He – for his part – refused to give the couple a second glance. Behind them were a few individuals, apparently in middle life, who were busy shovelling some ripe oranges into a sack. One of them wore a traditional hat, fluted like a stack, and of southern Italian design. All of these denizens – regardless of their occupation – slightly froze when the man who bore the family name of Borghese passed. Weren't they vaguely supposed to be aristocrats from up north? Surely a fascist magazine had once been called *Borghese*? Didn't a war-time photo exist of the count in naval uniform and sat next to an SS driver in a sleek limo? An image which could only have been taken during the Salo republic. It also proved to be reminiscent of Italian neo-realist cinema.

PART THE THIRD

With a setting sun behind his aspect, then, Gaati strode on with a jacket slung casually across his shoulder. To one side of him a peasant crowd has already gathered; well they knew his famed temper of old! A house on two storeys – albeit with rickety windows and a slate roof – loomed up at right-angles or in a hidden vertice. But Borghese looked straight ahead… as if nothing could faze him. Do you hear? His hair has been whitened by mainland imprisonment or care, and yet the features remain noticeably unchanged. For one thing the face is square, masculine, massive, slow, Cimmerian or Hyperborean – and incredibly violent. It betokens a combination of two sculptural types: perhaps these were the smoothness of Dobson's intimation concerning Osbert Sitwell… when spliced with a Paolozzi head.

An object – in the latter's case – which re-interpreted *Cyclops* (1957); or some similar spasm of the imagination. Might it bring back – no matter how severally – a painting by Graham Sutherland like *Head III* in 1953? Wherein the formulation of two eagles comes together in paint, and not necessarily after Russia's imperial house. Yet it's more to do with an alleviation of space in a situation where images coalesce – somewhat anthropomorphically – in light. Has one ever seen the transforming photos of Edward Muybridge?

PART THE FOURTH

The man walks on and his pace slightly slows the nearer he gets to the town's centre. Could a limp really be discernible now? No not quite... For he trudges on with a sense of inevitability or keenness after dark, but with his honour undislodged. Indeed, prison comes as a scant or even a necessary disgrace in this society. The buildings were old scale – at once lacking in grandeur and without any lofty ambition. Certainly, they couldn't be described as Romanesque or tending towards the grand, let alone the Imperial. Let's see: they seem to be typical for this part of the Mediterranean. All of them were white-washed and customarily blanched – with the odd cat lying sideways in the dust. At last, though, Frederico Borghese Gaati stood before the old family abode on a central thoroughfare. Its walls are constructed of solid stone – whether robust or ancient – and yet a tracery of cracks covers its surface. Might they represent (in one's personal mythology) the mummified features of a face dismally untombed? Perhaps – by way of a parepraxis – it recalls one of those sarcophagi in the British Museum, or a Bacon portrait which betokens dismemberment? Regardless of all this, the immemorial head of a crone comes silhouetted in a nearby square. May it be an example of topping-and-tailing; or at least cropping in terms of a photographic image? Because the hag's head appears to be in profile within the space; it looks out on the street timelessly, gesturally and without let or hindrance. Has she been on this corner, *ceteris paribus*, for a year, ten years, possibly a century or even a millennium? It matters not… since her face sags towards immemorial sadness, blankness, resignation, even embitterment… but without any check on a residual passion. She sits there waiting --- somewhat necessarily --- for some sort of an end… that is: a culmination, finish or checkmate. No mating can be expected from her lineage, to be sure! Moreover – and directly to one side of her on the left – looms a crucifix. It is large and Italianate; after the fashion of Cimabue's early experiments in this line. Don't you remember that these southern sacrificial marks were fleshy or toothsome… even vaguely sado-masochistic? Because they hint at the thraldom of Mel Gibson's *Passion of the Christ* (perchance); or a late Dali seen in reverse perspective where the crucifixion is viewed from above. Needless to say, the old crone's jaw sagged with a lively turkey-cock of abundant flesh… together with an ineffable weariness about the eyes. Yet these two – when set back in wrinkled dewlaps of flesh – also twinkled with happy malice! Her all-over dress was black, with her white hair tied back in a bun and a small crucifix adorning her neck. The house in which she sits and looks out from happens to be the home of his youth… somewhat after Pasolini's description of tearaways in the street. Furthermore, there was an immobility about the woman… a timelessness. She waits for aught – quite clearly – and maybe it's for this silver-haired stripling to stop beneath her window. What goes around comes around, as they used to say in the 'sixties. It must be karma, fate, destiny or the prescription of the Norns. Didn't the ancient Greeks settle here too? For tragedy waxes as old as this world. She reconciles herself to reverie --- to a beginning that's an end, to stillness… Here comes Gaati; an eagle circling its prey --- all of it taking place in one of Hades' fire-pits.

The sun's gone in; he stops in front of her.

PART THE FIFTH

"Bon journo, Signora...", he said with curt respect and just on the edge of insolence. "Does my beloved sister reside here now... or should I say still?" "No, Frederico... the bird has flown its coop, so to say. Any road up, her domicile had been elsewhere for many years... itself long subsequent to your departure." A slight gap intruded before the last word here. Might it be a hint of nervousness on the crone's part (?); or maybe a cough? Most definitely, her interlocutor bristled slightly. "But you remain doubtlessly unawares, Frederico. She scarcely rises before even-tide or the moon's rays, and then the girl goes abroad in search of men. Every *demi-monde* happens to be addicted to her men friends, don't you agree?" At this the Sicilian stepped slightly closer to a stone window ledge. Moreover, his massive fists found themselves to be clenched in a furious transport. Weren't they knuckle-dusters without metal (?); or otherwise redolent of great hams hanging down? To be certain of our ground, then, they betokened a haunch of venison --- itself a contemporary venue for post-modern art. Whereas, in this particular moment, Gaati's mood took off in a futurist direction – rather like Boccioni's sculpture of an *Object Moving in Space* (1913). Wasn't it sleek, untransparent, fluid like magnesium or indicative of Aries' fire? It encoded Greek Flame or a touch of the mediaeval tar-brush; albeit shifting slightly towards a four-dimensional livery. Frederico remained unaware of such metropolitan developments, however. He just claimed an ex-convict's status, after all. Yet Boccioni's 3-D vertigo – in its transparent gyroscope of flux – radiated a savagery which leant it a classic poise... hence its authoritarian nimbus. Furthermore, the elixir of right-wing art remains fourfold: it must preach the heroic, transcend, be hierarchic and evince beauty as power. Brutality is the finesse of a new statement, in other words...

PART THE SIXTH

Under his gaze's assertion --- my readers --- the old witch shifted back in her seat (somewhat uneasily). Yet, in her heart of hearts, she smiled secretly to herself. For truthfully, Belladonna wept tears of unrepentant joy; even though they came wrapped up via a mildly blocked aorta… insolently enough. Do you see(?), and you don't have to be her doctor to recognise it. Since what else can there be to do in a clime like this, other than engage in malicious gossip… especially if you're a wizened Erda. Similarly, Frederico's fists had tightened into balls, with blood pounding in his inner temples and maybe bereft of a forehead. He stood foursquare, a jacket flung loosely over his shoulder and one hook-like mitten opening & closing. Could it be considered a sadeian formula or make-belief; rather like a dissident version of Peter Pan? Or alternatively, Captain Hook has sprung alive from J.M. Barrie's pages! Nonetheless, a church candle – of the thickest imaginable yellow-wax – burned merrily away next to our whickered step mother. It tapered off before a semblance of bliss; even when stuck in a sturdy brandy bottle. While its smoke became convoluted, twisting and turning in the light as it moved in fortitude's arabesques. Belladonna waxes pleased though. She had struck home… All the time, as the ex-convict approached her portal, she had dreamt of being the one who told him. Behind Frederico the street moved away in a haze of smoke and bluish light; thereby illustrating the candelabra of its magnificence. Whereby the entire scenario – morally speaking – reinvigorated Rouault's painting *Aunt Sallies*; a canvas in which bride and penitent coalesce in paint as thick as Gilman's. May it delineate a semiotic of painterly abstraction; itself riven by religious judgements?

+

Here and now, the old trout almost backed off in the face of Frederico Borghese Gaati's ire. Steam issued from his mouth and nostrils, veritably so. Because the elderly female's face seems to be creased, distended and long-filleted… rather like a fish opened up from the side. Her triple chins quivered; primarily by bobbling up and down like obscene sands or obsidian clays. Strange it is how mortals at the end – when facing death – approach childhood yet again. Perhaps they crawl towards the cervix or innermost entrance; while abreast of a logic that pertains to Samuel Beckett's *Comment C'est*? "Don't look at me in a Cyclopean mien, Frederico", gibbered the oldster… "No, hee, hee… It's quite obvious: the entire town, replete with its white-washed stone structures, knows what your sister's been doing. She's a harlot, a whore; Frederico: a hussy who, after the fashion of Alberto Moravia's *Women of Rome*, goes with a multitude of men astride of a variety of positions." Was there aught wistful in our crone's vernacular; almost as if she is disappointed with her truth? Now that it stood unadorned in the dwindling sunlight. Maybe one can detect envy or procrastination (herein) --- even misstatement? Had the oubliettes of Krafft-Ebing penetrated beneath these geriatric lips and lines… only to find Stygia's spiders thereafter? Especially when a Sicilian evening portended (betimes) and lust expected naught from a vampiric twilight.

PART THE SEVENTH

But what of Frederico? On hearing the woman's words he'd almost passed into another dimension. Truly, the experience took him like a gust of laughter from without. Can it really have been a momentary possession? Possibly… yet a vortex of colour and lines briefly took charge of him – even in its leave taking. In this it incarnated one of Arno Breker's principles… despite having become subtly altered. For inside Frederico's mind a brazen torso reared up (instantaneously so). It rather revisited Praxiteles when crossed with a tensile steel-frame outside a restaurant called *Briganzi's*, in Soho, during the 'eighties. This was a monumental cavity or a Grecian body which knelt before Josef Thorak… presumably when crossed with Frank Frazetta's water-colours. Regardless of which – these gleaming examples of Leni Riefenstahl's *Olympia* found themselves self-reflected (rather reflexively). Wherein each image rebounded back on its neighbour in a combination or stasis; albeit after a parody of Rene Magritte's stopped reproduction. After all, each variant delineated a response from Arnold Schwarzenegger's 'Mister

Universe' adverts in the 'seventies… Yet underneath them came a swirl of black; whereas this major-league Apollo found its head encased in a blue cube. (The latter proves to be a square – at once sapphire rendered – that had been tendered from above).

+

"Tell me, Belladonna", enunciated Frederico in a much calmer voice, "where are these men to be found? You know, the ones who have occasion to visit my sister." "Or whom she pays attention to – when roistering in an abundance of peacock feathers", tittered the old woman. Maliciously, she found that she enjoyed her Cassandra role. "Look no further than the local taverna, Frederico", she enjoined. "There you will find ample evidence of their presence. The Gambasta brothers and their cousin Silo are always carousing in the afternoons. They waste many hours in those booths from noon till well into the evening, afore they venture out to visit your sister. Each needs to stoke up some dutch courage, you see."

PART THE EIGHTH

Her gnarled finger points percipiently into the distance… almost like a reptile's tongue which suddenly dashes from its slashed mouth. Ha! Ha! Are even her eyes closed and cold, like those characteristics accorded to the serpent folk? Yet who can tell? Because Frederico's slow, gestural mind has already begun to contemplate future business. Yessss… He will pay the Gambasta brothers – plus their itinerant cousin – an unannounced visit at the very heart of their carouse. Most appreciably… his jaw hardens into a granite-like repose. Also, the man's thick, slab-sided Sicilian face affected a certain wisdom… at least when seen in profile. Didn't it encompass a nineteenth century silhouette (?), although in thinking on't… such an ebon pitch lay beyond Michael Ayrton's *Minotaur*. Frederico has turned his head now in order to look outwards in the direction of a pinkish effulgence: the former limned before a light-blue stingray. You see, throughout his audience with the crone she had been resting in a rickety, balsa chair. Whereas he was at head height beneath her looking on. Moreover, a sudden flash comes into our imagination: it was John Piper's painting of a classical row in Bath, Somerset Place, which has been smashed to pieces by bombs. It took place in 1942 and yet it indicated a post-situational folly: or *the culture of the ruins; the ruins of culture*. Yet Stewart Home wouldn't be able to 'smile' over this discourse, since Belladonna's stone-swept room has about it the antecedents of a transcendence. (Note: a while back, in Margaret Thatcher's nineteen eighties, Home ran a communist and nihilist magazine called *Smile*. It advocated an art strike; a notion that totally backfired. He also sought to promote radical materialism, Dada stunts, conceptualism and proletarian praxis as the way forward in art. His failure was total. It's best to think of him as a more inverted variant of Andy Warhol who seeks fifteen minutes of fame minus Solanis' bullet in the gut! Bravo!)

+

Inside Belladonna's room – if looking aslant at it – one can see a bare stone-wall which sweeps up to the open window. On this a spartan table had been placed in order to accommodate her modest fayre. It consists of a bottle of red wine, a flat Sicilian loaf and a large cheese. Perhaps it might have been flavoured with aromatic herbs? But, in any event, a triangular segment has already been removed from it and devoured. An ornate or circular painting in a frame – vaguely reminiscent of Caravaggio – adorns a darkened wall. While sombrely (and in the foreground) one detects the iconography of a saint, looking vaguely like Father Christmas with a long white-beard & holding a crucifix before him. It subsists in a peculiarly shaped booth that holds it upright… thence adding a sepulchral essence to this scene in dwindling light. In the farthest corner, however, a slightly modernist sculpture intrudes --- somewhat incongruously. It incarnates a heroic car fender or a colophon when cast in the format of two Futurist wings. They seem to beat the air with the havoc of an abridged cry!

PART THE NINTH

Frederico Gaati has left black-garbed Belladonna behind him. He strides onwards with a merciless purpose and thinks only of a coming vengeance. The excitement mounts to fever pitch and yet he remains superficially calm. Abreast of his head what's left of a darkling sky has been peeling down – albeit in such a manner that just leaves a residue of French blue. When looked at formally the hilly structure of Sicily's terrain becomes observable. Whereby ribbons of white-washed walls curve away over hill-sides… each one of them adjacent to the next in segmented squares. Moreover, the natural cascade of this terrain causes these various divisions in the land to coalesce as far as the eye can see (somewhat artificially). Varied steps – often made out of massive stone-slabs – provide walkways or ecological stepping-stones up and down. How little this atmosphere had changed, when one comes to consider it, from the island scenery described by Giuseppe di Lampedusa in his novel, *The Leopard*. Granted: Frederico Gaati remained oblivious to much of his surroundings, concentrating, as he was, on an inner vision. Again, one factor became noticeable amongst others, and this has to do with the modulated stone roofs of Sicilian dwellings. Each one faced off against t'other within a preponderance of sun, given the likelihood of these white-washed forms to melt into light. Since one factor stood out above all others: and this is a sun-beam's quality or its unreality. It became simultaneously effulgent, pellucid, etheric, self-reflective and transcendental in its forgotten glow. Does anyone reminisce about that painting by Hieronymous Bosch; whereby angels, recumbent to a cone, float off into Light? One also has before us an example drawn from le Corbusier's architecture… rather necessarily. Given the fact over whether this ultra-modernist, who designed several churches or chapels, sought to three-dimensionally convert various Cathar and Albigensian edicts. (Especially when one recognises the SS intellectual Otto Rahn's exegesis in this particular area). These involved an obsessive search for Purity; at least in terms of a pure solar glare which led to a desire to transcend matter by making it into lit-up motets. A doubly perplexing feat (this) when one remembers le Corbusier's love of pure concrete: itself spiritualised through an upward striving and while adorned in white paint. Might chinese white from a tube sublimate brutalism?

PART THE TENTH

Still, Frederico Gaati strode on with a merciless architecture apparent in his spine. Whereupon he passed by these white-washed dwellings which were glimmering in the sun or filing out in a seawards direction. Occasionally a small stone window – albeit tiny in terms of the wall's dimensions – poked out from an otherwise granite sweep. All of it occurs under some louvered roofs – themselves often orange or misspent, and sloping down in undulating folds. Small tufts – of irregular grass and shrubs – lingered roundabout. Gaati does a blitzkrieg like Guderain or Liddel-Hart's tank theory. All of it comes to illustrate a late Dali – such as *The Hallucinogenic Toreador* of 1969-1970 – where a half-naked Venus morphs into red and green. Are these not the colours of Eros, at once transparently forgotten? Surely the buds of a new enclosure, *a la* winged flies, just crept out of this dream's portal? Even though such a filter of insects insisted on coming through a cone of sand, against which a numinous head finds itself reflected. Stone pillars also play a part… they reconnoitre the periphery of Lacan's habitation; only seeming to broach a renewed psychiatry (thereby). Since a toreador smites with golden meat by basically flailing in sunlight and at a time of these fruit-flies' decapitation. No mercy will be shown such *Drosophilae*, you see: as they turn --- in comparison --- to silver. During a moment where a mathematical correspondence merely conceives of future decay by means of numbers – particularly when it's adjudged in dots. May it residually betray Op art's burgeoning tendencies?

PART THE ELEVENTH

In profile, however, Borghese Gaati has altered little from a *Soprano's* adolescence... albeit in a traditional Sicilian vein. Yet if we look closer at this then deeper grooves can be discerned. These marked the temerity of his features; a situation wherein a distorted truculence came to be observed. His etching was craggy or untroubled – after the unflustered magnificence of some rock. May it really be described as a force of nature; the likelihood of which reared up from its own resource after a Hyperborean keepsake? Similarly, a token of this landslide waxed chthonian: almost as if they had come up out of the ground. Can you grasp it? Since Gaati's lumber-jack essence or withheld intrigue seems peasant-like, super-masculine, ferocious and dour. It certainly exhibited a lugubrious mien – directly after the sword-and-sorcery images of Frank Frazetta, and delivered in water colour. The hair – in turn – has long ago filtered into grey, so as to articulate a semblance of its dying. No Grecian 2000 had been used here! But still, the eye-brows were bushy, thick and black. Already though... his flaming blue-eyes were looking back in time, as if they were addicted to a cornelian passage between dimensions. For, unbeknown to all, Frederico Borghese Gaati's mind dwelt on previous or past instances... where a slight to honour could only be punished by death. Abundantly, he remembered his slaying of Umberto Eco – not a semiotician but a fisherman – who'd allegedly ravished his sister. Wearing a pair of loose-fitting sandals, Gaati's younger version had stabbed his moustachioed victim through the chest, while wielding a clasp knife at the time. Large it was and double-sided: when Eco's blood spurted in a lively fashion over Gaati's hand. Whereupon his traditional Sicilian hat spun off into the evening's light like a revolving cartwheel. Furthermore, at such a decisive instant, Eco's orbs gave up the ghost by becoming two pins... both of them concentrating on the near-distance.

+

Did it illustrate that climax to von Stroheim's *Greed*, in a screenplay where McTeague and his assailant, Marcus Schouler, finally come to blows? All of this bursts out amid the suffocating heat of California's Death Valley!

PART THE TWELFTH

Our attention now shifts to Gaati's trial for the above offence. The southern Italian district judge is summing up. May this entire imbroglio have taken place during the reign of a certain Iron Prefect? Anyway, this official looked at our 'man' from behind reinforced spectacles. A chain of prefecture or administrative discipline lay around his neck. Might it have dazzled what Nietzsche once called, in *Thus Spake Zarathustra*, the pale criminal? Yes assuredly, but perhaps our attention becomes transfixed on the policeman to his right. He stands there gnomically and after the fashion of a forgotten sculpture; with a double-chin resting on a blue compartment or space. Necessarily so, for behind our Judge's receding hair-line, when slicked back with the sheen of a felt-tip pen, we observe stain-glass windows. Like in a domed architectural design they are, with many individual pieces of mock-frieze making up a plaster. Each sector of resin reflects a multi-dimensionality; *avec* every shard then becoming overwrought in comparison to a spectral imprint. Doesn't a ray refract from such dexterity rather prismically (?); and in relation to the cosmetic beauty of Newton's experiments? All of which came to be characterised in H.T. Flint's *Geometrical Optics*, when this professor was serving in the physics department of King's College, London. Most availably… Whereupon the judge, Bernadotte, announced in full pomp: "Frederico Borghese Gaati, do you have aught to say afore my Court pronounces sentence upon you?" To which the accused answers in a baritone voice. "Yes, your Honour, I must stain the silence with a flame's effulgence! Certain matters of family honour can only be settled with a sacrifice of blood. Haemoglobin – in such circumstances as these – remains the kaleidoscope of our forgotten years. Biomorphic excuses, pertaining to Lombroso or the social causation of liberal utilitarianism… neither of these are enough. I must answer with the crimson that flows from a poniard unseen. Isn't it reclusively obvious? My word, the pig Eco befouled my sister with his tongue and pizzle; his life, therefore, most high Judge, was forfeit by virtue of a family's pride! No humility shall be canvassed in order to still the necessary outrage of one's blood. When I murdered him I slew not a man… but merely a slobbering carcass. In the human abattoir, I had just to hack off a porcine head and place it on a sharpened pole during those hours of darkness in a barn. Torches, when held aloft in concealed niches, then flickered all around and sent boiling fire out into crevices. Do you profit from the quiet recesses of those damned?"

PART THE THIRTEENTH

During this performance, Gaati stood perfectly still and he was dressed in a dark open-necked shirt. Yet the face waxed slab-sided in its openness; at once resplendent with a prognathous jaw, dark black-hair and a steely impediment in terms of an eye. Indeed, this orb flickered in its socket like a marble… although it proved to be subdued of all light. It dwelt upon the scene engagingly, raspingly, totally, as well as minus any moral conscience or doubt. It evinced – most convincingly – the serpent folk's cruelty! Does one link it with a glassy lustre so as to see?

+

By way of contrast, Judge Bernadotte appeared unperturbed. Truly, the heavy solemnity of Plato's *Laws* lay fully upon him… albeit foursquare and abreast of a day. Can this be in order?

"Frederico Borghese Gaati, I hereby pronounce sentence", he rasped. "This has to be a society of Laws, Frederico, if we are to raise ourselves above the conduct of beasts. Can't you grasp this salience, eh? If your beloved sister was harmed by the fisherman, Umberto Eco, as you attest, we possess laws to deal with his kind. It isn't for you to take on the arbiter of judgeship. Are we to have a situation where – after the collapse of Hoxha's Stalinism in Albania – criminals took over a lordship's apparel, robes and ermine? All such rabble, like a revolting tribunal, sought to impose vengeance upon their fellows. It cannot be permitted, do you hear? Otherwise a condition of anarchy shall prevail, and it will fail to be the Utopian vision of Bakunin, I can tell you that flat out. Now Frederico Gaati, no suspension of disbelief may be tolerated, whereby mountebanks were suspended upside-down by meat hooks. A series of events which occurs in abattoirs or yards, especially when mobsters take up justice's remit. Does one recall the antics of the Richardsons... a conspiracy in south London? In truth, jurisprudence betokens the mulled wine of sages. In this instance, private revenge cannot be allowed by our island or its government, even if it claims tradition's precedent. Pertaining to your case, the people's voice isn't divine... MINE IS! No law of silence protects you from the fact's brutality! Therefore, this court sentences you to ten years in prison... the expiration of your term must be served on the mainland."

PART THE FOURTEENTH

During his outburst, the Law-giver took on a nimbus of inhuman *gravitas*, almost like a character in one of Aeschylus' tragedies. Yes sir. For his jowls were open and aghast, or they merely quivered before a bulldog's advent. Also, the chain around his neck came into more pronounced notice... when interlinked with red. Behind him a swathe of black eddied around – possibly after an artist's indentation or involving the brouhaha of William Nicholson. Never mind: since the Judge's face turned upright in a garish transport; together with an adventure in grease smearing the whole. His eyes squared down coolly, officiously, and with a temperature of indifference. Could they be seen to envelop a saturnine venom behind those 'fifties National Health Service spectacles, and by virtue of damnation's utterance? An orange tie led off from the neck; at once cut off aslant its leash and exhibiting a future gibbet... presumably out of tune. Without doubt... Because at the moment when Frederico Borghese Gaati was 'sent down' a flourish of Edgar Varese's music came into court. It inundated the whole with *Arcana's* spectrum (so to say);

thereby leading to ultrasound's reverberation along some metallic sheets. Further to this, two burly policemen led the convict from the dock, while beneath his feet various ancient flagstones kept the participants from the court's well. A crowd has gathered there. Nearly all of them were anonymous, whether male or female, with upturned faces of apportioned glee. Some affected disinterest; whilst other persons, nursing unknown wounds, gazed on in discrete satisfaction. Suddenly a commotion occurred in the outer precincts of the court. A disturbance had broken out that was pronounced enough for officers to call it to a halt. Yes… divers blue-and-grey uniforms gestured across a bay at the public end of the court's gallery. Wherein a slatternly dressed sixteen year old girl has chosen to stand. This must be Frederico's young sister, Suzy Travolta-Imray Gaati, about whom all of this trouble had gathered. She lay across a public balustrade with her arms outstretched and tears rolling down her youthful face. Might she have something about her of the coquette, perchance? Any innocence came knowingly and even with a definite price-tag attached. Her blouse or slip rose up around her; momentarily tightening over all the right places. Whereas an exceedingly short skirt skimmed or slanted astride her rump; thence revealing the proportioned legs beneath. At the farthest side of the court-house lay a bench, the length and plenitude of which seemed to mark it out as a specimen from the ancient world. May it have been Etruscan in its lineage? Anyway, Suzy called out plaintively: "No, no, never… it's against nature or natural right. They can't punish you in this way, Frederico!" To which he replied, with the policemen dragging him thither to start his sentence: "Refuse all tears, little sister. I regret nothing, having done it for the family honour. You'll have to encompass feminine bravery. I intend to return, most definitely, in a decade's motoring."

PART THE FIFTEENTH

Ten long years have passed in silence. One can only think of it as a very pronounced disturbance or continuum, especially in an otherwise sleepy Sicilian hamlet. After all, the ministry of health way back in Rome configures an average male's life expectancy to be fifty. That's right: a man who reaches maturity here counts himself lucky to notch up over half a century. How then, in such shortened circumstances, can Frederico let bygones twist in a southerly wind? He marches sternly down a side-street with jutting perpendicular walls rearing up on either side. Doesn't he stride between them with the demeanour of a warrior, possibly an aforementioned centurion? Could he be compared to Longinius, the one at the mound of death who comforted the slain with a spear…? Its outermost tracery had been dipped in vinegar, primarily so as to quench thirst's necessity. But no – when one comes to think on't – the event's converse cannot really be Golgotha: due to Frederico's kinship with one of the two thieves. Rather… the death's-head which chooses to subsist here (sic) refers to one underneath the skin in an Elisabethan way. Certainly though, Gaati betokened more of a soldier than the majority of male specimens roundabout.

+

Speaking of which, two men amble out of a taverna or a neighbouring ristorante. One of them is an ordinary working-man who wears denim trousers and a sheep-skin jacket. He has over his upper lip what can only be described as a 'seventies moustache. A small 'proletarian' cap sits jerkily on his shaven pate. He greets the traveller with cheery gusto… "Eh Frederico, long time no see, huh? All I can say is welcome home." This elicits no response whatsoever, whether of endorsement or hostility. Whereas another individual also hoves into view. He must be considerably older than the other two; thereby evincing a desperation that can be seen in his drunken and shambolic gait. This bag-man lurches towards Frederico – when seen from the back – and he wears some sort of jacket which is distilled from fading green plaid. One arm comes thrust forward ahead of the other and this was almost to make a point in terms of a plundered windmill… all of it occasionally observed in bright light. "Frederico", the stranger announces in a loud voice… virtually as though he's welcoming a long-lost brother back to the fold. "Don't you have a few precious liras to spare, young one? I'm a bit short myself at this time, like. Do you choose to remember my weather-beaten face; at least when held up to the elements like a parched manuscript or map? I chanced to be a good friend to your father once, even though many moons have passed since his journey. Only a few coins, I ---". "Out of my way, you indelicate swine!", roared Frederico Gaati… virtually thrusting the oldster from him with his vehemence.

Now alone, he chanced to visit the taverna. Its vast wooden doors swung open and led to a saw-dust strewn interior. Whereas the stone trellis-work of these massive blocks leant a heavy and solemn lustre to the atmosphere. There was no futurist lightness of touch after Marinetti's quixotic alertness; merely the lugubrious ochre of Giotto's pictures. Recomprising Levi's diction, Christ may have stopped at Eboli… but he had certainly not come here in the dwindling light. This had to be altogether reminiscent of Chacha's contemporary silences, labyrinths and conspiracies. Wherein walls meet walls, all of which lead to dead-ends or faded out perimeters. Everywhere a Mafia lurks unexplained. Frederico Borghese Gaati then enters the bar with a slight jauntiness in his step. *Lex talionis…* for Gabrielle D'Annunzio's lore of erotic violence lies heavily over this particular scene.

PART THE SIXTEENTH

The returning convict sits down heavily at one abandoned table. Doesn't his giant fist lie upon the table-cloth incongruously, rather after the fashion of a great joint of meat lying astray? Wasn't there – in turn – a late biographical work by Stanley Spencer: namely, the one with a ham before each other's flesh? It could be described as an example of John Martin *avaunt* a French butchery dealing in horses. Under this glow, Frederico Gaati stared moodily into the nether distance… a cosmic radiance gleaming in each eye. Throughout this performance

Frederico's face was set in a saturnine whisper, with the lower lip curled or pursed in morbidity. While the jacket which he had carried with him from the quayside, once slung over his shoulder, now found itself propping up a chair's back. At the furthest end of the bar an oil-lamp gleamed in its silent space; thereby casting a pale effulgence or glimmer. It worked out the mosaic of ornate brick-work further up the bistro, and vaguely hanging over to the right. Lifting up the bar – when viewed from diverse angles – a crowd of drink-sodden men stand at right-angles to one another. Didn't their nethermost bodies or torsos recalibrate rectilinear lines drawn from a Vorticist composition… say, one by William Roberts, for example? Take – by way of recollection – a work like *The Arrival* by Nevinson which hangs in the recesses of the Tate Gallery. Or why don't you choose to compare it to a composition (of percussive depth) by William Roberts known as *The Diners*? In it, a constellation of guests in some London eaterie are observed or find themselves otherwise shot from the air. These oblongs or rectangular shapes embody a new incarnation: somewhat after the encryption or secret code of Wyndham Lewis' *The Wild Body*. Might these le Corbusier blocks reconnoitre a new prospect or fade out into pure light; at least when resolved to avoid skin and bone? Occasionally, one of these men lets out a sigh, a burp or a belch. They often embrace or tug at each other with their claw-like hands… even though a glass is raised aloft, now and again in the bar's twilight, to some imaginary victory or conquest as yet uncertain. These are the Gambasta brothers (most probably) when accompanied by their cousin, Silo. Mayhap various other hangers on, who are drawn from the town's byways, help to make up the numbers. Do they represent a ravening wolf-pack or a baying switch of hounds, save only in the helplessness with which they go abroad? All of a sudden Frederico becomes aware of the place's odour; that is, its combination of sawdust, sour wine, mouldy bread and worm-eaten meat. It adds a tincture of disgrace to the abiding discomfiture… Whilst, moment by moment, our anti-hero's gorge is rising. You see, he has come to realise that the rage within --- the furnace inside --- may only be stilled by vengeance. Isn't this Vendetta's land, perchance, with a capital V working its way up to a disconcerting silence? No John Cage will live here amid these twinkling clinks or green glasses, since only the sound of a belly laugh can be shattered with a knife. Meanwhile, a young girl with jet-black hair has approached our main man.

PART THE SEVENTEENTH

It is completely obvious – from the most casual perusal – that she doubles as a waitress by way of a prostitute. Her name was Cazana and she nears this mastodon's table without trepidation. She vaults up with an improvement's nymphomania as to dress, plus a high-lighted bodice which keeps up those cups. A light flimsy top comes spread across her front; at once aerial to the confounded breasts within or otherwise provocative to those ripe melons that lurk aslant. Amidships, a tight black-skirt covers her extremities; themselves teeming away towards vice with the deportment of those legs. Whereas the skin betrays the olive complexion of a new beginning; it's abundantly inside a grave and adjacent to Sarah Young's pornography. Can one see? Anyway, on either wrist subsists various bangles; each one of them Gypsy-like or vaguely disreputable in their ormolu. A rolled-gold character this happens to be; the likelihood of which jangles on any available pole. While her sylph-like arm pretends to stroke the underside of one of Frederico's limbs; the latter contained within a stainless white-shirt (as it was). Well! This gesture has about it an insincere cast that's possibly enlivened by a scintilla of *Eros*; the nimbus of which exists underground or abreast of a subterranean fire-light. Frederico Borghese Gaati had never beheld Alban Berg's opera *Lulu* which is based on Wedekind's play. (You're not able to tune to Radio 3 in an Italian prison camp.) Nevertheless, he'd have grasped the plot; even the dithyrambs of *Messalina* in Albert Jarry's non-pornographic deliberation concerning this story. May it forever rest in peace with the surrealist movement!

+

Cazana spoke to him in a high tone rather like a serpent, but slightly tremulously and with a lisp's undercurrent. "Dear one, how far you have travelled by way of evening and out of all night-times. May one detect the outcome of this Stygian offering? Or – if impossible to witness – does your heart roil upon the dust like the shiny complexity of a thousand scales: all of them amber to a golden nectar? Do they instaurate the vision of a million whores who float freely or abreast of a gigantic moon (?); rather like the earth-mothers of Albert Louden's pictures. Yessss… they are sibilant after a serpent, you see? Nonetheless, many an eel will shed its skin in this Garden of Eden, no matter how prelapsarian. Because a harlot's basilisk-eye finds itself painted around the mouth; or, Mary Quant-like, it delves into an eldritch liner. Whereupon a thick cobra thrashes around behind a screen… thereby delivering up a quandary of red and green (variously). While – atop this vista or auric sensuality – a beautiful Grecian mask appears. Might it specify a Goddess' lustre out Aphrodite's way (?); a mask which strikes one as perfect in its inhumanity."

+

Our lantern-jawed Sicilian gives his answer without looking up: "No Assyrian raptures will imprison me within an iron maiden's draught. No sir. Since the superhuman – when masked and without pity's raiment – steals the show behind an emerald valve. Does one detect on its front the heavy mosaic or scarlet arabesque of an Eastern extraction? No matter how toxic this perfumed air may prove to be… Regardless of which – our golden mask reinvigorates a thespian enclosure that's given over to Eros' silent violence. Masturbation is only the improvidence of dwarves! Especially when we realise that this beauteous mask grows out of a snake or a lithe copperhead's nectar: the undulating spasms of which thrash and thwack beneath one's shield. All of a sudden the lower jaw of the helmet falls down; primarily so as to give up a new ghost's dispensation… in terms of projecting a dark square. Yes indeed! Then it says one single word in an unknown *argot* or Esperanto: "Come!" Out of all due vehemence of which – I grab hold of a broadsword and swing it in an arc in order to decapitate the asp. When my blade severs its head a great torrent of black and red blood spurts out. Do you see? Gobbets of its ichor – the Gods' sap of yesteryear – gush forth like an Icelandic geyser. It inundates the whole and yet I am unperturbed. For, like Norman O. Brown in his psychoanalytical treatise *Life Against Death*, I have sided with the flames against the flesh. Mark me: Abelard was unrelated in his vision and retained a castrate's wisdom to the end. Because you are determined to whore --- whilst I wish to resist in accordance with masculine fury. Isn't it so? Furthermore, the snake's snout – when bedevilled by its Grecian mask in gold resin – flies off only to leave the barrier smashed to pieces… given the convulsions of this constrictor. Surely, you are aware that in Indo-Aryan civilisation or ancient India one of the God Vishnu's incarnations is a five-headed python? I've cut off this phallic monstrance…"

Cazana: "Do you require food, wine or possibly aught else?

Frederico Borghese Gaati: "No; nought more than bottled Chianti… and then some privacy, sow."

PART THE EIGHTEENTH

Yes indeed, the afternoon drags on and it translates into a diurnal rhythm against the embers of a light outside. Does one choose to detect it now? Truly, the Elisabethan imagination chose to call it the skull beneath the skin due to a delicacy in its use of poetry…

Shades of dreaming
imprisoned in flesh
seemed to walk across this room…
without a steadfast interval.

For doesn't the door to tragedy lie open (?); primarily through impermanence's lustre or an abattoir's sluice. Surely the Belgian surrealist Felix Labisse, a member of a faction misaligned with

Andre Breton, went to paint in slaughter houses? It added a sadean allure to distemper's after-effects – whether they were mindful of pain or not. Possibly – and in another dimension – Cazana glides across the polished floor… she is a testament to the fact that radiation can turn sand glassy, (*inter alia*). Also, she stepped gingerly along… particularly when dressed in white's virginal waspishness and with a zodiac laid out beneath her. No matter how tremulously this Pope Joan couldn't escape from Dennis Wheatley's influence, albeit on a floor of ebon marble. Behind her, or in imagination, there reared up a dais of the fondest blue under a sacrificial canopy… plus various candelabra poking up here and there. While ahead of her blank dress – whether ethereal or diaphanous – a polar bear-skin lay upon the floor. Its head was attached and it looked grizzly, gnarled, toothsome or bloated (all at once). On she laboured across the architecture of these floods… with the primal lurking beneath the surface of an innocence abroad. It had more to do with Gabrielle D'Annunzio than Robinson Jeffers (admittedly); but a link remains intact regardless.

+

The afternoon wore on and it became later and later – by the by. As it proceeds, the panes on a flat window which is opposite wax darksome. It possesses the word Cinzano the other way round and impregnated in the glass; at least when seen reverse-ways-in or reviewed from the restaurant's inside. Eventually, the brickwork of the bay becomes lost in sombre tones – itself a mural that's suffused in a sulphuric hue. At the bar various derelicts prop it up… each one plastering a toast to Venus' lips. Several half-consumed bottles of wine lie open on the table and sundry glasses surround them. Each one of these looks to be stained, greenish, red-tinted or reflects an amber translucence in its dwindling light. The occasional wine-stain is observed on residual boards; themselves smoking heavy-wood and lying laterally across such drinkers. All are lost in their abundant carouse or binge; and they pay no heed to the smouldering presence in the corner. A scarcely touched loaf lies before the

Gambastas… possibly a cob, it's hardly had a knife or butter through it. The clan concerned were blood-brothers or kin; themselves being leery, boastful, lush, fervid and distastefully libidinous. Some wear small or pork-pie hats; while others are clean-shaven: with the sole exception of short moustaches over their lips. A few have rolled cigarettes in their mouths' corners; whilst they manifest a variant on dress' disrespect or self-neglect. A shambolic mien heralds their advent or dharma; yet none of them can have any foretaste of the coming shambles.

PART THE NINETEENTH

During these darkling hours, our brethren become more and more drunk… while the atmosphere liberates a bilious urge. Peevish and inebriate chortles are heard throughout; particularly amid the guzzling of wine down these collective throats. A heavy, lugubrious drizzle dampens the air… if only in our imagination and as wine fumes cloud one's senses. Could it revisit a scene from a von Stroheim film before cutting (?); where in *Queen Kelly*, a degenerate marriage takes place in German East Africa. (This later became the British protectorate of Tanganyika after the Great War, 1914-18). Whereupon the wedding occurs in a brothel or a bordello, and it is superintended by a guardian's dying body. The ceremony was performed by an African priest who – in reality – proved to be a white man blacked up… a visage which possibly recalled the leather solemnity of a mask! Anyway, it has Al Jolson associations as well as indications of inferiority, the 'Bell Curve' and deliquescence. Haven't moderns ever read Count Arthur Gobineau's *Essay on Racial Inequality*? To sum up (though): the intended spouse in this decadent union was to be played by Tully Marshall… a past master at von Stroheim's vaudeville. While farther in we notice that low-keyed lighting, hanging drapery in niches, under-lit booths and religious icons all contrive to create an atmosphere of *Grand Guignol*. Prostitutes – who are done up lasciviously and lick their lips continually – also attend this anti-nuptial. When we consider that their eyes were painted basilisk-like, their lips wax ruby-red, and their extended finger-nails happen to be long and tapering. A later novel – published only in French and called *Poto-Poto* – distended this theme in order to involve the presence of siamese twins. It all exemplifies a loveless marriage; at least when seen through the degeneration theory of Max Nordau.

+

Soon after, the Gambasta brothers – together with their nocturnal cousin Silo – start to boast about the group's 'romantic' exploits with Frederico's sister: Suzy Travolta-Imray Gaati. Such voices gather up a thick lament; at once coming on strongly in their glottal-stop immediacy. Each raises a glass to the absent other - -- only to see it capture the light of a deluded sun. Never mind: since Frederico notices every last scintilla… as sundry impediments slouch across the former's arm or with a bar between them. His eye revolves and swivels like a chameleon which catches at the dawn of a new leaf – but it misses nothing via a rotating retina. One Gambasta merges into another; primarily by dint of appearing square on whilst toasting an absent *demi-monde*. Whereas Silo stood ramrod straight against the rampart of a linear saloon. Drinks – or frothing wine bowls – were then handed around betwixt these votaries at an obscene rite. Yet during such moments – and unbeknown to them all – Frederico Borghese Gaati noted down whom he had to kill. His knife came whetted on the far side of an indifferent culling, you see.

PART THE TWENTIETH

The time for a muted cavil has ended now. Whereupon action, in circumstances like these, came to the fore as morality's unction… but the Gambasta brothers (plus Silo) were well away and they thought nothing of boasting too much. "A toast, my belly-ache or ilk", leered one of their eldermost sots. "Let's give voice to a gesture of tongues – particularly when we bear in mind that Suzy is the *femme fatale* we all desire. Isn't she the caprice of a rutting antelope who falls foul of those Roman ruins to the town's north – and under a boldly red moon?" Again – in a twinned dimension – a vision enters into their deluded minds… it might well concern Sally O'Hara in von Stroheim's *The Merry Widow*; a girl who artificially raises her skirt in order to attract attention to a stocking's rent. All of the male eyes are drawn to this leg's length; at once lithe, tensile, black-garbed and supported by a 'Manhattan Follies' packing case. Likewise, what is one to make of a reclining Greta Garbo in a version of Pirandello's *As You Desire Me*? Where von Stroheim, whose presence in the cast Garbo insisted on, looks down upon her as the novelist Carl Salter… In a tableau in which her voluptuousness or cheese-cake situates itself beneath his head and stick. Could there be a recurrent motif of a penis in a vagina less precise than this?

+

"Listen to me", insists one of the Gambasta boys, "do you remember the orgy scene with Prince Mirko in von Stroheim's *Merry Widow*? Here various naked nymphs lie about – basically by sporting eighteenth century wigs and black masks. These were eye-piercing gestures around the head; albeit after the fashion of Baroness Orczy's scarlet pimpernel. It all hints at a counter-enlightenment where – after the service of the poet Robert Lowell – de Sade's *One Hundred and Twenty Days* becomes a negative encyclopaedia. Do you berate this gesture, somewhat suggestively? Remember the following, comrades… Suzy Travolta-Imray Gaati leads a man forwards against an orange background; and she's black-haired to a jet or ray. She wears a jerkin of blue cloth or serge; together with lycra around her loins and boots at either end of those extremities. Don't you detect the sun shining on their glistening surfaces?"

PART THE TWENTY-FIRST

Now Frederico decides to make his move… in a gesture of tumult whereby his eyes glisten with a saturnine lustre. Didn't the female wolf suckle those who were destined to found Rome? To which mental extremity Borghese Gaati gives voice: "Those who have sinned will be blasted to their souls' depths! Do you recognise the entrapment of a wolverine's cry? Because any outrage to family honour – like the atonality of Varese – calls out to one in a manner reminiscent of blood streaming from Abel's body. Yet Durer's engraving comes reversed out on our graph. For – herein – a pile of heads arranged in symmetrical pyramids isn't necessarily the way to go. Since Cain's mark upon the forehead (if placed there by Providence) will not deter us from the Chapman's art... dealing, as it does, with Goya's cryptic after-glow. One only cuts to the heart of a meaty residue; therein to discover an emptiness which delivers no peace. Certainly, you recall the last scene in von Stroheim's *Greed*; a situation wherein, and at the epicentre of California's Death Valley, one character catches up with his nemesis armed with a six-gun. But I require no such tool." With this statement... Frederico Borghese Gaati lays about him. The clasp knife flashed forwards or to and fro in a hemicycle of sprinkling gore: the like of this spraying a trajectory of meat. May it represent some anti-art event or 'happening' in real time from the nineteen seventies? No: this all happens – whether staggered and at issue – in terms of a Circus of Horrors that we have a ring-side seat next to. First of all, we require a close-up on Frederico's eyes: the character of which glistens with a recognition in those depths. None of this prevents the blade's cascade, though. For doesn't it recount a struggle between the spouse and an admirer in von Stroheim's *Blind Husbands*? Wherein a scream or yelp offers up blood only to find its 'teeth': themselves betokening a loss... All of it then exists behind an abattoir's front. It is more a question – resultantly – of what subsists adjacent to a red rather than *the* green door. Inescapably now, a gnashing of alms evidences even in its truculence... and each Gambasta screams while poniards enter their bodies. These are divine pass-keys or sigils, both in their rodomontade and delight. Frederico luxuriates in his violence... at once freed from norms and bourgeois conventions that take place even in prison. His combat-knife licks out simultaneously; thereby slicing through the Other's carnival or fun-fair. It speeds a hot restiveness and unease; thence carousing with spleen or nonchalance. Giblets continue to fall in their locution – thus splattering forth upon an unclean floor. While heavier men who are long out of condition in Sicily's taverns blunder about a light-stage. Soon they were down and suppurating from a thousand wounds… many of them conceived in the imagination. Conceptually speaking, it relates to a splicing of Damien Hirst's taxidermy with Albert Metzger's auto-destructive art! Can the iconography of one particular piece – like a two ton bronze by Henry Moore – be stolen for scrap metal? Anyway, Frederico Borghese Gaati towers over them; and in a tableau of rheum he brings alive Lorca's blood wedding. (This was long before the Ulsterman known as Ian Gibson set out to explicate it). Granted: each sliver of mutton articulates Ares – when covered in gore or undefeated by Homer's drum-beats. [These were those very same 'commando' slides in a Doric language about which Blake had complained]. But such earnestness is behind our hands or swipes, since Scylla's topography enters in. Could it enliven a circus that occurs possibly on Bristol's downs or Birkhamstead's common? Might an expanse of land – when covered with undulating craters and hollows which make up Peppard's green – come in handy? It burst out from its portmanteau called the 'Dog'; especially when we bear in mind that a pub of this name lit up such a village. Gaati remained oblivious to all these wrap-arounds, but still a vaudeville like this continued on regardless. It harried the facts from beyond one particular barrier. For a sun-wheel revolved in its oscilloscope amid mayhem; while repeatedly waiting to drown out nothing else. First and foremost, these big-dippers took no-one for a ride or adventure; whether over dunes or forgotten apple-cores. In one circle various figurines tumbled pursuant to Dante. They cavorted with besport and lustre. Our mountebanks walked up and down poles *avec* each one balancing on the other's head (depending). Or alternatively, men climbed up ladders after a fashion which illustrated ships' rigging. Perhaps one's childish pursuits came emblazoned on it; when relative to a spinning top's whiz? May one even summon up from memory the board game known as 'snakes and ladders'?

Still, no mugwump concocted putty from such a cripple's locution. Do you notice its vagaries? Further to any aplomb like this – these individuals dance the line of a renewed Apocalypse. Whereupon hominids who were dressed in the finery of Edwardian gentlemen rolled Bradley's cigarettes whilst balancing on the trapeze. All in all, it waxed lyrical concerning a high-wire act. Could it be reminiscent of Angela Carter's *Nights at the Circus*, perchance? But the aftermath of this anatomy lesson becomes clearer now… and it relates to absolution or silence. Because not even the tortured science fiction of Ray Bradbury or Heinrich Boll can save us here. No way… since each denizen must fall beneath an encrusted knife which pleaded about a forgotten intention. Certainly, they leap up and down circus ladders for support – each one acting up under the other's prominence. Whereas a wide-sailed vessel makes its way across such longitudinal poles in between these bouts of popular jargon. Do you see? Further – in another necessary incarnation – a Phileas Fogg character who sports a main-frame moustache vaults his cubicle or rises up behind a stone effigy. Similarly, various other contortionists perform on hobby-horses or nodding donkeys… the latter resting from their proper purposes. Each jumps on a gymnastic theme only to swivel atop its tubular or mechanistic fare; and all of them revolve on a catharine wheel armed with white candles. (Note: the major producer of such illuminations in England is Carolina from Lindal-in-Furness, Cumbria).

Soon all of Frederico Borghese Gaati's chosen assailants were dead or dying.

PART THE TWENTY-SECOND

Their several corpses, which were pickled in their own innards, lay in complex or interrelated heaps. One clutched at a table-top – when abreast of a mushroomed spore that quickly ran to its source. Like Dali's oneiric method, it was all over in a minute and with Frederico side-stepping the challenge of his magnificence… if only for a moment. Are you born to be dead before the liveliness of this fate? For his 'Eyes' found themselves plunged into a pitiable misstatement – wherein indifference's locution presumed on a drunken spree: what with saliva and sweat ceasing to be at home. One man *avec* a tail-end of beard lay groping over an upturned table; while another curdled at a desk. Reddening table-cloths --- once of a brilliant white --- now lost their lustre to an oncoming suffocation of scarlet. Similarly, the flood-tide of this anti-balsam did nothing to relieve the show; especially when we recognise that every sound has been choked out save an occasional gurgle. A light-trellis or a grid subsumed Frederico in its glowing aftermath; whilst over in a corner quivered the harlot. Her entire world-view has basically rearranged itself forthwith; so as to consist of nought but petrifaction or due states of fear. Do you remember any concordance with James M. Cain's *The Postman Always Rings Twice*? Or, even more appropriately, the expressionist film starring Peter Lorre and known as *Mad Love* comes to mind… whatever it may have to do with Andre Breton's novel of a related title. In this filmography the past-master of Fritz Lang's *M*, Lorre, pursues a beautiful starlet up a cylindrical staircase of expansive width. A Freudian locution --- or what? Also, as she screams and screams in terror or panic, her dress trips her up… only to have her grope step after step with high-heels defeating a climb. Meanwhile, Lorre decides to discard a black hat and coat – both of which have become an encumbrance to his pursuit like a ravening insect. Now, he proceeds to reveal himself in his full glory – and rather like Gloria Swanson at the end of *Sunset Boulevard* – he's delivered up to the keep. Immediately, he snatches off his face, and it peels away like a mask in order to reveal a metallic trophy below. Is he more a machine than a man, albeit after Asimov's machinations in *I Robot*? Likewise, all our pulchritudinous floozie can do is yell and yell in a high pitched tremolo! While – all the time – his touch gets closer and closer… when given the absence of an expectant curse. Whereas all of a sudden his very arms and hands fly off; the latter stretching out to reveal prosthetic limbs so as to pat up the stairs on a limber's distortions. Can't you tell? It is characterised as the plasticity of a rubber man, but this instant those disembodied mittens caressed a bottom tightly held in a 'forties skirt. Don't you register the sound of Ruby Murray here? All these milliseconds, however, our babe continued to howl like a hyena who's feasting on tissue paper.

PART THE TWENTY-THIRD

Simultaneously though, Frederico Borghese Gaati moved across the taverna in order to grasp this whore. Not for him the blandishments of an empty white-screen... wherein events are played out after a carnival's patterning. *No*. His response to perceived reality was to beat it into a bloodied pulp. Against this – or in terms of its confirmation – a condottiere version of our circus ceased to level its pulpit. Whereupon various mountebank occasions tended to orate a passion in which a duchess swings from a hybrid frame. She was wearing a toga throughout. Or, by dint of grief, such tumblers trip over each other's heels... even if they revolve around a King of the Fair. Most especially – when he wears a crown of maple leaves or crumpled paper, irrespective of those chairs or wicker samples he balances on. Alternately, a lone and spiralling indent – when naked save for a loin clout – spins on a tormenting wheel... the latter embedded in the floor with a heavy impress. To one side of his rotation (and espied in a Dantesque masque) stood a tormentor in a triangular hood. Might he have been a klansman or a Dominican who was withering to a rootedness of sparks? Meanwhile, two neo-classical sculptures embraced below and they were both partially disrobed. Each one could be considered to be part of the Elgin marbles – whether male or female – and characteristic of signalling either Anchises or Aphrodite.

PART THE TWENTY-FOURTH

By notification of the above, then, Frederico Borghese Gaati grabbed hold of Cazana and twirled her off her feet, or possibly around about. In this, she represented a puppet character like Giselle in one of Eric Bramall's marionette reels. Furthermore, the two of them spin around in a devastated continuum – at least when viewed from above by an aerial shot. To the north lay a man's prone body and his non-designer shoes sport a hole… while, all about him in the gathering gloom, a red liquid saturates or wets these boards to a burnt-sienna costive. Accompanying this to the south, a white hand lies restlessly at bay – it refuses to move after the fashion of those horror films where a severed pinkie makes hay. Roundabout our dramaturgy vessels of mayhem quickly deluge one's senses – what with broken bottles, glasses and chairs backing up a fountain that squirted nothing but blood… like in Iran. The flag-stones covet an irregular dignity; and each one kneels to the side when viewed mathematically from on high. Great pools of liquid lie stagnantly or in disaggregated combinations… some of it alcohol by way of an unholy ichor and deluging into sap. "Please, NNNNNOOOOO!", screams Cazana. "I've done nothing disrespectful (now); or pertaining to not finding a straight target for one's arrow. Might one narrow its witness, thereby? Don't slay me, I beg you a thousand fold. You see, the character of a golden-coiled snake has to be Stygian or ebon, and it's wrapped around itself in a pewter bowl. Doesn't the outside of this dish betray the presence of axes and mallets? Necessarily so, since one can beat upon the surface without impinging on what lurks within. Terrible in anger, (it is); whilst dreaming lotus clouds of rapture or hidden within a reptilian haze. Could this constrictor or youth be dreaming of a muscular consort with green skin… plus long-flowing locks which contrast with red-specked eyes? Yes truly, it betokens a saurian correspondence: the double-agent of this sensing a new identity in its split-eye, somewhat reflexively. It's a mirror…"

Yet throughout Cazana's trebling or trembling Frederico keeps silent, (ominously so). Now he speaks out of clenched or gnashing teeth – like the dialogue in a Roman Polanski film. "No pitchfork can pattern this pig for slaughter… because all attempts to fatten it have fallen before one final hurdle. Rest assured, I have pitched up most mightily against filth's reservoir. Yes indeed, now inform me, strumpet, what I've occasion to intend… namely, where resides my sister, Suzy Travolta-Imray?" During the course of our Beauty & the Beast's encounter, (sic), the slab-sided entourage of Frederico meets a Medusa full in the face. Has one ever recorded the advent of Jean Cocteau's faery tale in 1945? Similarly, the girl's *Skin 2* breathes nought but the air of one of L.S. Lowry's waifs; and she comes up close to Gaati while feeding on Ann's ubiquity. Are you free to loosen such a moment's shackles? Still and all, each visage closes on the other's absence – what with her black hair flecked behind them or reminiscent of a snake's threshing. Might it be a copper-head's example – albeit when necessarily taken outside of Keneth Robeson's fables? Her dewy eyes gaze into his retinas… while his granite protuberances --- jaw to chin --- resemble the crenellations of Mount Rushmore in terms of many a U.S. president. Both sets of lips are full, heavy, succulent and just given over to a reprieve's absence… They also happen to be very Mediterranean in aspect. "Tell me what I want to know", exhorted Frederico. "Cease your inconstant babbling… woman. I must ascertain the truth about my sister's embraces or their ready longing before the Gods. Do you remember that sketch from von Stroheim's *The Wedding March* – itself pursuant to an arranged marriage where a butcher takes his ebon-tressed bride to an altar? A dais of blood it proved to be – after a sequence which is drawn from a Japanese *Macbeth*. Again – on such a template – we can see a husband's virtually psychopathic stare for the occasion; it appears to come right out of a Colin Dexter mystery. Wherein a bald man who exists in twilight searches desperately in the night-time… could his tonsure be rendered next to Elgar's music? It happens to be Christmas eve – but any thought of an eleventh hour has long been suppressed; since the minute hand's strayed past midnight. December the twenty-fifth had now emerged; and yet this desperado continues to feverishly hunt for some object dropped in the car. He carries a pencil torch in order to illuminate such a scene*. (*Editorial note: this realisation has been taken from life). Given all of this… instruct me over finality's judgement and in relation to some modelled tints. Were they really delineated by von Stroheim (?); and do they look up into this camera's priest?"

+

Suddenly, the Jezebel known as Cazana breaks cover, if only by way of speech. "His hair was slicked back… but the eyes stare maniacally above the moustache. They glisten like two ball-bearings; at once hardened to ultra-sound or teak: while his white dress-shirt, suit and tie hasten to nothingness. Furthermore, the audience behind him glares on… and they react like grotesques who are drawn from an Emily Dickinson poem. Each one looks on --- essentially being statuesque, hieratic, judgemental and even sequined." "My sister, wench", instructs Frederico Borghese by way of a bluish prism, "what of her?" The *demi-monde* responds thus: "Every night she waits or dotes on the ones you have slain. Although who takes the dominant or submissive part – when relating to an active or passive principle… who dares say? You comprehend my meaning, eh? Right enough, big boy, she yearns for those gentlemen and paws the ground like a wild beast up by those Roman ruins to the north of town. Irrespective of this, though, a scene from von Stroheim's *The Wedding March* indents meat's purpose – where a rape nearly occurs in a butcher's yard. It's a pictograph abreast of which a haunch of venison – like in Francis Bacon's *Painting '46* – hangs down from a pink alcove… rather resultantly. It blunders on to a renewed lustre (thereby). Likewise, this playlet's visceral nature transposes 'it' onto such a wedding… thence causing it to feast on an endless rapture. In Suzy Gaati's chamber, then, she not only requires their presence or support, but stays with them until the morning's light."

"You LIE!", snarls Frederico.

PART THE TWENTY-FIFTH

The Roman columns loomed up before him aplenty and in a forsaken glow. A latter tint suffused this edifice with magenta's onslaught – while merely swivelling to gold or otherwise capering off with a full moon. Assuredly then, flakes of the sky seemed to circle in their orbit; thereby rescuing them above or planing down to various lines that subsisted in the heavens. An orange pall hung over the stone-work – albeit correspondingly blanched to its white conspectus and tapering away in terms of a mock-Circus Flavius. How, in all honesty, can it be compared to the gigantic construction over in Rome? I ask you! Don't you conceive the curvature in its spine? Anyway, this Imperial power – which was redolent of the Caesars' gifts – attracted down to it the Rock's ambit. It hung in the sky like an asteroid aplenty and was almost full in a near-planetary sense: with the outer pits of its surface becoming obvious for all to see… Let us notify such a grave-time as this; in that its spheroid architecture became arbitrated upon via many a moon-flight way back in the 'seventies (no matter how unwillingly). Aren't there those who maintain in a *Fortean Times* way – and contrary to the given facts – that such moon-landings didn't take place? Also, can one repair to or even remember those Moon globes with mortal names appended to every mound… as enacted after the lineage of Sir Patrick Moore? Furthermore, this disc – with its sovereignty over menstrual tides – always indicates feminine power in a manner that's reminiscent of a tarot's indulgence. Doesn't it embody those heavy, stagnant waters of a scorpionic vengeance? Whereupon heavy water – as delineated in David Irving's *The Mare's Nest* – comes to mock at the transcendent and this was by way of dragging all thoughts back to matter. A toy-theatre (this) wherein they wax embroiled with earth or its tidal onrush; and let alone an emotional cataract of blood. *Frederico Borghese Gaati has never known it to congeal on his knife*!

+

He dimly recalled the events in the taverna before he had occasion to vacate it. Didn't the scarlet woman, Cazana, taunt him to his face – rather like the prostitute character in von Stroheim's *Walking Down Broadway*? She was played by Minna Gombell in a project later reshot as *Hello Sister*. Regardless of any of this… Frederico pushed her to the stone flags below and she became convulsed by a fury reminiscent of a sound world like Vaughan Williams' *Fourth Symphony*, for instance. Nonetheless, Cazana blurted out: "You fool! Haven't you been away in gaol these long years… in order to adapt the terms of Jack Henry Abbott's *In the Belly of the Beast*? Suzy Travolta Imray Gaati's decadence is unparalleled. None can approach her *apropos* her orgies --- at least not myself. Do you remember the incidence of it in Guccione's *Caligula*? When they contrived to reject Gore Vidal's script; a document which certainly wasn't based on Albert Camus' play. To witness it:

She roiled like a tigress
naked before a marble throne
with ebon eyes flashing –
and in a saurian complexion –
after dusk.

While her long dark-hair came dishevelled halfway down her back. Don't you hear the rustling of a serpentine access in the grass? It's post-lapsarian, after all." To which Frederico Borghese Gaati responded in full pomp: "Get away from me, transgressor! To me, Cazana, you are on a par with the Congoid beetle *Mecynorrhina Polyphemus* who pushes a lump of dung through ripe fronds in the savannah. It remains difficult to have any through-put, however, and this is why 'you' must roll it sideways via multiple revolutions. I have spotted your degenerate game. It levels you up – point for point – with an Anglican priest's son known as Genesis P-Orridge who was once of the new wave band *Throbbing Gristle*. He is now destined to change places – transexually – with his own wife. Infamy, get thee behind me… satana!" Frederico then pushes her violently to the floor. She stayed there panting and heaving for a while; *avec* her bosoms trembling as he stalked from the bar. A solitary bottle of Luxton's Irish cream lay off in a corner – all by itself – during his exit.

PART THE TWENTY-SIXTH

Beneath Frederico's boots a river flowed sweetly; its waters lapping in a lambent way around neighbouring rocks. Various bushes were lit up by fire-crackers and each one sprouted up from the earth – what with Rome's ruins staring down at a watery islet. It was at this point – and spattered with gore from his murders – that Borghese Gaati came upon a recognition… namely, he must cleanse himself. One after the other his massive fists opened and closed. How may he receive his sister – sweet, innocent Suzy – when dressed with an executioner's overlay? Truly, he must douse himself and allow such crystalline rivulets to flow across his musculature. Not being high school educated, he wouldn't realise that one cannot embrace one's martyr-sister when covered in entrails, or after the example of Arthur Honegger's modern opera *Joan of Arc at the Stake*. These were surely the innards upon which Tiberius' soothsayers had fed; especially when existing up on buildings like those ruins that towered above in a darkling grandeur. Let it be said: his cries and entreaties were premature; or of a prior moment. They echoed remotely or with resonance around those coping-stones – let alone such monoliths to excellence as these. What has he really ventured now? Why, it caterwauled with masculine indulgence… but not spleen. Culturally speaking, it reconnoitres the sounding-board of one of those Futurist machines which were superintended by Marinetti (in retrospect). Yet the voice had more to do with a deep bass than a soprano – never mind Mario Lanza or Enrico Caruso. "Suzy, Suzy Gaati", he'd yelled… It was a call out of nowhere and by dint of twilight, or in pursuit of a candle-light's filter upon a blade. "It's me, Frederico, your brother… I've come back in order to protect you, darling, like I uttered in court. Isn't it so, eh? *Capice*…?"

+

Frederico Borghese Gaati then drove suddenly through a watery skin; thus penetrating the icy pericarp while tasting deeply its chill. Almost naked now he washed in mid-stream – albeit with his hands above his head and a torrent of water subsiding off one of Praxiteles' frames. Around Thorak's after-glow some rocks loomed up or became cloaked with geologic lore: and they 'lusted' to replace sandstone with granite… themselves being constructed from basalt. Again, by virtue of a summery expanse some green foliage limned the hydrogen oxide; thereby filtering the moon's aspect or tilt… --- As this orb appeared in the sky; at once interplanetary-like or floating above, and possibly hardy and sulphurous… even stuck to the sky like a pitted disc. What was such a noise? At first he didn't recognise this sibilant or dulcet sound, but finally he realised that his sister is calling to him from above.

PART THE TWENTY-SEVENTH

Instantaneously then, Frederico rises from the churning depths within which his form has been subsumed. He breaks the silvery surface so as to momentarily gain greater purchase on his sister's words. Rising like a dolphin in the ghostly brightness of eventide, his head cascades under a shimmering water-fall with every last drop flitting to its accustomed place. Moreover, this liquid bout decants away over a curtain: with each passion or droplet of it striking out on its own *avec* adolescent lustre… mote by mote. Is it a deliquescence; or more precisely a pulsating rainbow of steel? It certainly exercises the pointillism of an unknown brand – particularly when looking above or savouring each spectrum of colour, wavelength by wavelength, in terms of Newton's shards. Yes… This incandescent prospect has to be Blue in pigment: at once prussian, ultramarine, pthalo, cobalt, cerulean and brilliant. It also occurs by hindrance of some green and before such a panorama fades into turquoise. Yet Frederico's heavy, masculine, Cycladic head looks up askance or in awe at what transfigures its potentiality ahead. Whilst his outstretched paw – when cast by Michelangelo on a rainy day – strummed the lake's surface *in lieu* of skimming coins.

+

A sweep of tundra or an ochre rockface divides Gaati from the sister he's so avidly sought. Ought it to resemble a revelation drawn from Rider Haggard's novel *SHE*? Never mind: for this clay then danced a saraband under a moon's reflective glare. Suddenly he spotted her (!); when delicately etched or silhouetted against a Sicilian asteroid. Didn't Professor Moriarty – presumably an Italian exile – make a name for himself with his thesis on *The Mathematics of the Asteroid Belt*? Who cares, already? After all, Frederico never bothered his grey jelly with Italianate academe: whether it be over Croce, Gentile, Eco, Morante, Evola, Praz, Vasari, Gramsci, Paglia, Lombroso, Pareto, Freda, Machiavelli, Pavese, Malatesta or whomsoever. No way… But what stood out for him was the shadow or the articulate nimbus *a la* Jung which flitted across our spheroid. It curved like the beak of a vulture in spate and it encoded a golden eagle in darkness shaking her wings (rather alternately). Does one recall the portrait of Henry VIII's falconer – by Holbein – that was inspired by the habits of Renaissance or Italian princes? Is it a matter of Castiglione's *The Courtier*, customarily? Frederico Gaati continually shook his head… Because – for a moment – he suspected his sister of having wings; else how could she have escaped his notice or arrived so unexpectedly just now. The night swept or limned blackly behind her shape.

+

Indeed, Mario Puzo's *The Godfather* has nothing on this… Listen to the following, my brethren: Suzy Travolta-Imray Gaati loped naked across the turf. Wasn't she divided into six (mayhap); and in accordance with a representational oil-painting by Bob Larkin? Wherein dark brunettes who were wearing nought but G-strings and tinkling breast-plates besport themselves across grey flags. Also, they cater to ankle guards about their extremities as well as various amulets; together with bedizened necklaces and other adornments. Suzy could throw herself forward within the twinkling of an eye or dance herself into a frenzy… signifying Salome's only twin! A consummate actress or performer, she might hurl her body to the ground in a transport of abandonment or lust. A compact entered into not just for male approval, but also as concerns her own pleasure. The eyes, meanwhile, betokened a basilisk stare: at once mascara'd, lined, over-painted and sporting a dalliance with gold. Each orb has lashes attached to it which were themselves dark… Yet, on occasion, where were those cat-like pupils? Did they manufacture an emptiness in the retina? Since, *inter alia*, these white eyes lacked all wondering or mirroring effects… Truly, Suzy Gaati came hither. She opened her mouth to speak; and out of it waxed a tinkling bell or the music of forgotten spheres. "My brother, Frederico", she lisped. "You have journeyed far to come upon my ageless body here. Hearing of your hunt I would have zeroed in to your task, had I not been searching for my friends…" With this dolorous ambit, she turned her back on her brother and looked away across the island. Next to her left foot and nestling close to the ground a hedge-hog or a vole squirmed clear. It seemed to have fallen from her *talons*. This little creature made away at full speed… somewhat reprieved. Neither brother or sister paid it any attention whatsoever. She shook her black hair menacingly. Rather abashed – and holding his clothes before him – Frederico Borghese mounted the slope. The pre-eminent thing he noticed were her tresses. They extended from her scalp to her buttocks like an unending black lava from Catania or its flame. She evidently cast no shadow on the ground… or so it appeared. One long-nailed hand massaged a hip with a skewed leg; while another continued to flick back her hair like a disabused and growling tigress. But no noise declared itself save a low whistle. Frederico approached her drawn by a sylph-like kindred – as was vested in the lithe body before him. Her frame etched towards a silvery hue in this moonlight; the latter coruscating up and down her pulsating envelope. Borghese increasingly became aware of the musk, frame and glowing perspiration – never mind blood – of the womanhood he'd defended. She spoke again rather more defiantly. "You betrayed us… me… the Gaatis when you killed my 'boys'. Having learnt this I became very distressed, Frederico, do you hear?" "I had to", squealed her sibling almost after a character in a Verdi opera. "They defiled you by their breath and presence. Massacring them turned lyrical (you see). It became one's elixir of moral goodness. Their orgiastic boasting sealed their fate. Don't you agree on our mother's grave, eh? Fate offered me no choice but to grasp vengeance's dagger." Suzy Imray found herself sitting now and she was partly obscured by a shadow which fell across the classical façade. Next to her – Pompeii-like – rose a cut-off Doric column. Phallically, it half raised a sprout rather impotently towards the shore. Can one remember Bulwer Lytton's novel known as *The Last Days of Pompeii*? Her relative – for his part – stood with a man's legs open before her and his clothes came crumpled at the breast; as well as the fact that he wore only a loin clout in this silvern hue. A mosaic or the patterning of a frieze intervened between them in its solitary stone. Travolta-Imray's fingers kneaded it convulsively and uneasily. She cut the atmosphere again with speech: "No, no, no… oh my brother, Freddy, you have it all wrong or turned base about apex (no matter how suggestively). You see, a transformation has been wrought in me these very years you've been away imprisoned on the mainland --- by Hecate! A sickness, an aberration or a malady afflicted the town… No-one knows for sure; but it could have been faulty blood transfusions or batches of diseased plasma from the United States, et cetera… Haemophiliacs of the world unite; you have nothing to lose but your chains! Didn't the Refoundation Party of Marxist-Leninism once say it? HA! HA! HA! HA!" She laughs suddenly and it's like the tolling of a monastery's bell. It reinterprets a Berio oratorio which is possibly sinister to hear and that catches hold of her like a force from without. Frederico jumps slightly… the first time he's shown apprehension on this day of all days. "No, spawn of our mother's womb like me, no-one may degrade us. None will ever successfully drag your sister into whoredom's roils. For merely human standards leave me bereft – now that I AM A VAMPIRE!"

+

Presently, her face is seen against the moon's solid entity and Borghese hadn't noticed the canine incisors over ruby lips before. Suzy's black hair cascaded behind her and the witch's planet shone clean or sheer – while atop our vixen's head she wore an Etruscan mask. Theatrically, it bore upon its cover the *Agon* of Greek theatre… a factor by no means unknown to Sicily given settlement from the Peloponnese. Each eye-slit has about it Clytemnestra's cruelty in the *Oresteia…* at once fervidly delivered in those nets and adjacent to one's bathing. It is then that she leapt and carried her brother's body over the frieze. He hardly has time to scream… whilst Suzy Imray ripped out his throat with her vampiric teeth. Both of their bodies caromed together nakedly or breast-to-breast. They hurtled to the ground with her tapering nails pawing convulsively at his back. She suggestively wore an ormolu arm-bracelet around her upper limbs. It's the sort of useless detail your mind registers at this hour! Her body – when leaping like a diver in Leni Riefenstahl's *Olympia* – crashes into his. Over they went. Her hair embraced him akin to a crone's all-enveloping shawl; itself darkly ebon. The last thing Frederico Borghese remembered – as a red and black sludge inundated his eyes – was the fact that he didn't die alone. For another Gaati enjoyed revenge as much as he did. But surely a vampire's victim returns as part of Polidori's brood? "Now brother", whispered Suzy Travolta with a mouth full of gore, "you shall share my lusts!"

THE END?

WILDERNESS' APE
a vignette

I
Hadn't Haiti been an island or a fierce dependency of one thousand drums? Assuredly then, its rivers or islets measured the green across its length; and each curving bay of this fumarole's shore maximises one's strength... Customarily and again, the whole came livid with a lush undergrowth – even at a time where the leaves' wetness proffered many advantages or it hints at a hospitality to do with the jungle further in. Do you begin to protect this truth? Since – when viewed from the air – our republic's trajectory lay like a dead seal on its side... at once covered in trees and with the odd promontory jutting out perpendicularly. Nothing comes of this repast – but the water lapping around its extremities swam clean or it flitted like a silver-back's entrance... The semblance of Dr. Moreau's island in H.G. Wells' essay on vivisection, and known as *The Island of Doctor Moreau*, seems relevant here. (N.B.: This is never mind mentioning Brian Aldiss' later rendition – by way of a sequel). Still – to one side of this phantasy – stood an African mask which has been carved out of bark. It rained on the perimeter of its frontier with ovals for the mouth and eyes... and by dint of a zero's native signs. What does a Fool tell Lear, but not in Edward Bond's travesty of the Bard? 'Nuncle, thou art an O without a figure; a nothingness'... or suchlike words. Here one can ethnically spy its resolution in this aboriginal *summa*. Is it primal, nocturnal, secretive in its blatancy and otherwise hailing from Cameroon in West Africa? Let's be sure in witnessing this that it doesn't possess two faces; i.e., one in front and the other behind in order to ward off animist spectres which are all stalking one's back-line.

II
Revilo P. Oliver's book *The Education of a Conservative* has an essay on Haitian politics, but our tarot predicts an entirely

different 'Papillon'. Nonetheless, our tale begins with a powerful voodoo priest or Houngan who had his eye on a foxy mulatto girl… that is: a twenty-one year old who was pale-skinned in her miscegenation. But – in truth – mightn't her circumference turn out to be blue-toned; at once dark and sleek or with the affidavit of a female Pharaoh? Since the vixen's body and breasts were perfectly proportioned, or otherwise modelled to a purple bodice that barely covered their globes. It glistened under artificial light; together with a yellow surplus coming in-between the magenta trellis of this underwear when worn outside the body. High gauntleted boots fetched up to a steel livery – or they reached in the direction of those thighs so as to provide a surplus indication over Krafft-Ebing's art. Do you recognise the folly of what follows? Is it real? Certainly, a red-cloak fitted her hour-glass magnificence --- itself cast in synthetic sapphire. Even though it was in her hut that our shaman has come to pester. May his equivalent of 'sexual harassment' be at all congruent with Eckermann's anthropology in his tome *Voodooism and the Negroid Religions*? Now none can register it other than in a turquoise architecture that rises cybernetically overhead. In this incarnation or alternate dimension our animist becomes violently changed. Furthermore – without being untoward about it – he's best presented as a roebuck who had been vaguely humanised and with antlers sprouting from his skull. Truly, didn't the lead singer in *Laibach* (which was the rock band of New Slovenian Art) wear a metal helmet across his cranium… the latter replete to a sprouting stag? To be better qualified over this, though: it projected from the head when adjacent to those slit-eyes and both of them appeared to be ochre in tint. Moreover, the creature's heavy musculature seemed golden by way of its chest; and it was possibly glistening or even translucent. Whereupon a colt 45. – the most powerful hand-gun ever made – came slung from a holster and it ran from one shoulder to the earth's trapeze. All of which occurred despite the fact that the twenty-one year old from Marbial on the island rejected all such advances. You see, she was betrothed to another man – buck or no buck! Wherein her eyes glimmered; and weren't they transient sockets without pupils or fit only for machinery? The lids are almost non-existent when one comes to it; whereas an eyebrow arches up spasmodically or like a curving steer. On the other hand, an orange disc revolved on her forehead's panoply and it kindled towards an arranged jewel. Could it embody a Hindi mark which is just opening up to the pineal eye (?); a conception that enables everything to be laid out before it. Her skin, however, returned to cerulean and it lay shorn before respect's artificiality thereby, or it found a contrast to those beautiful white teeth. This was not to mention such perfectly engineered red lips; themselves modelled on Kate Moss' indulgence and which smiled without mirth. Again, the Houngan found his crude proposals repulsed by the girl; especially when this bint scratched him down both cheeks when armed with female talons. The voodoo priest – who had been humiliated in his pride – promised vengeance.

III

Exaggerating his loss – he then moved to enact a poison-pen letter and this was despite a debatable level of literacy. Alone, he enunciated a ceremony in its votaic fastness; and he thence sacrificed the black-and-white cock to a bowl of liquid flame. Its pitch let out an acrid smoke which star-dusted to sulphur. It billowed across this subdued chamber… while, at his back, there lay a white dais. Atop it symmetrical ivory candles burnt down towards their stumps rather like a cripple in a George Grosz cartoon(*); and they were also made from fine white-wax. (*One that could be said to illustrate John Gay's eighteenth century romp, *The Beggar's Opera*). To one side of this burning tar – and *in lieu* of a cauldron – rose a Benin sculpture made from wood. It combined features of timber and leather, you see, while it contrived to muster two faces: one came behind and the other ahead of its markings. All remains clear now, yes? His 'nemesis' proved to be a ritual sacrifice which is basically bathed in blood or gore, and with one dark mask over-sweeping. Its sockets rotated cylindrically or in terms of their absent perspective: plus one line merged into another not after Ben Nicholson's impediment… but more like Paul Klee. Does one remember, with some satisfaction, his painting devoted to infantile distortion called *The Possessed Girl*?

IV

Yet – having said all of this – the terrified waif or young girl found herself face to face with a mutant in another dimension. Might this embrace one of those miscreants or *residuum* who were plumbed by Cesare Lombroso in *Criminal Man*? Yesss… Assuredly, the mugwump's face leered up above hers; thereby excoriating or sifting: and serving remembrance's sieve when made out of gelatine. A colt. 45 was held menacingly against her temple and its barrel looked like a dull grey squint – while she dreaded any of its distant discharges. How this delinquent gibbered with glee! Truly, it depended on one's interpretation of Beauty and the Beast – but not necessarily after Jean Cocteau's roadshow in the nineteen forties. This much remains certain. Yet rescue may be at hand; especially given the mitten which this scarecrow covered her mouth with. Even now a dull ache developed across her face's lower side at this remembrance. Could we detect, soundly and in front, a refutation of Peter Nichol's disability play called *A Day in the Life of Joe Egg*? Never mind… since with one tremendous blow the armed mutant was hurled into a wall. It neighbours the summarised action. He then screamed and found himself upended from his feet – together with a black mouth which is open and casting rheum/plus various red eyes. They glowed like motorway cat's-eyes in the upper casement of his skull… no matter how emaciated each one turned out to be. Whereas the creature that assaulted him had three arms all part made of metal… leastways down one side of 'its' body. Who was this rescuer? Can it be a positive feature of the Houngan's lust, by virtue of defying all dualism? Because this vigilante bounced a rapist's brain off brick – only to prevent genital exploitation – or an exposure of what our Girl Friday didn't wish to see!

V

Having been cursed by the Houngan's voodoo, our wench collapsed soon afterwards. Passing through some island bushes which were all verdant with emerald, she immediately felt a constriction or malady… only then to fall head-first on the loam. It was almost as though life's breath had been forcibly expelled… as if by magic? Soon after her family's women gathered around with tears in their eyes, in order to place a muslin sheet over her corpse. The material was light and diaphanous – if unaccustomed to any fleece. Eventually it covered the half-breed's entire corse or dead body. Multi-dimensionally though, her three-armed saviour made some shift towards a lift door. It lay somewhere in a graffiti-bestrewn block and it hung on its hinges. (This walkway served as one of le Corbusier's contributions to rats in mazes, albeit thanks to 'sixties urban planning. Didn't they call it renewal?) Moreover, isn't spray-painted 'art' just the under-class' psychic vomit – contrary to Dick Hebdige's *mores*? In this respect, it institutionalises the psycho-art of Jean-Michel Basquiat: a Congoid, thief, juvenile delinquent, rent boy, sub-Genet hoodlum and AIDS wallah. The photographer Robert Maplethorpe later fixed him in aspic as an effeminate mattoid (primarily). It somehow revisits Eric Mottram's post-modern study of William S. Burroughs which was known as *The Algebra of Need.*

VI

Yet again, our three-armed mutant ran towards a closing lift; when this was itself illumined in half-light. Whilst at this door's basis stands our Blue skin, who was essentially as beautiful as the day she was born. But – when one came to think of it – had she actually been conceived at all? Furthermore, the power source over the escalator exists elsewhere and it subsists deep within a trajectory of marble… or virtually at the earth's core (nethermost-wise). This sapphire Nefertiti – with her breasts almost out – then stands with Three Arms on one side; together *avec* the roebuck who's merely haltered in green. While two rodent-like muties squeal and squawk during the lift's descent... each of them proves to be delicately unobserved. Have they ever read James Herbert's *The Rats*, perchance? Nonetheless, their eyes remain rubiate oysters in their shrunken heads. "EEEK-EEEK", they twitter and thrush – as the elevator goes WWWWHHHOOOOSH! It descends vertiginously and with incredible violence towards Jules Verne's radial.

VII

Now then, the 'community' became distressed by a death in their midst and all of her family subsequently visited the communal shack... primarily in order to inspect her cadaver which was freshly minted. Oh yes: each generation of a bygone tribe wept before this bier – as prescribed by Sir Francis Galton. Whilst overhead a flaming oil-lamp revealed a flickering scene... all of it in accord with our transposition or overlay, however, as a blue-skinned goddess, a roving buck and three-arms ran through a wrecked corridor. Surely it recalled – if only to our distant witness – the public housing development once spoken of? Certainly, our mutant (who possessed turquoise eyes aflame) now held a revolver to the mulatto's head. But wait a moment... weren't the bi-racial and our ultramarine-skin the same: or *alter egos* of like purport? Anyway, on a sordid staircase within this condominium the mutant and his victim huddled in the shadows. Next to them – and by way of Burroughs' *Last Words* – came two rodent stalks who each grasped at a revolver, but with peeling skin around their shrunken skulls. In the face of such a sapphire's sphinx (though) three-arms let rip... in other words, he fired his hand-gun without let or hindrance. (Doesn't this remind us of John Milius' group named 'Armed and Literate' – itself within the National Rifleman's Association?) Irrespective of which – a double glass-plate in a neighbouring window shattered under a tear-gas canister's impact. Despite the fact that a phthalo nymph – with her breasts half out over a golden bodice – leads this Comus Rout to safety abreast of a sudden cloud. Her scarlet cloak sways next to her in the breeze; while two mutants support a wounded man-stag. Hadn't he been shot earlier in our dreams?

VIII

Throughout all of this, however, the bereaved in-laws kept their dignity… even though extreme poverty meant that the casket ordered didn't fit its intended target. This wooden entrapment came up too short in order to pass muster as a Procrustean bed (you see). Where did our Caribbean island's deficit really originate from, then? Basically, it has to do with genetic insufficiency *a la* the creative nerve of Jensen's and Eysenck's researches – themselves primarily involving the latter's *Inequality of Man*. Whereupon a foundation IQ of 70 rising to 85 after inter-breeding, *ceteris paribus*, just carries a preponderantly dysgenic vibe. All of this results in 'Papa Doc' Duvalier's shanty towns not being able to reach a requisite level of civility – much after Lothrop Stoddard's analysis in *The Revolution in San Domingo*. Further to which – any attempts by revolutionaries of the south, like C.L.R. James, to discount this through revisionism ends up becoming deflated by endogamy. Hence we are left with Haiti's status as the poorest and least advanced isle in the West; i.e., a conflation of acute misery, cardboard dwellings, reverse evolution, AIDS and gang violence. Supervising it all, though, the Voodoo cult floats freely in a smoke-filled ether.

IX

The Girl Friday (in her death-in-life experiences) now dreamt a phantasm from the skull's inside going outwards… somewhat radially. After all, what can it be like to number among one's acquaintances a zombie… or one of Haiti's living dead? Similarly, this waif conceived of a shadow-sylph who lay next to her sleeping sister… what with moonlight streaming in from an adjoining window. Do you perceive its square configurations rebounding mathematically from a lit wall (?); or otherwise cast in emerald. Dimly, she remembers confronting her mother at a time when she held a teddy-bear in one hand. Slowly, oh so slowly… the adult woman rises from a prone position where, most significantly, the sylvan outline or inner sinuousness of her body recalls our blue Venus. An explosion is heard behind them and it just lights up an aperture with Greek Fire – a device used by siege merchants during the Middle Ages. (Ask any reader of Sir Walter Scott's *Ivanhoe*, for example!) Don't we observe a kind of bourgeois sentimentality here – which was best illustrated by Landseer's animal portraits from the Victorian age? Yet, in a final miserable tableau, the large bay windows open and thus move outwards from within… in concord with a lateral motion. This inferno looms up majestically and aslant her retreating mother… albeit virtually after a silent cinema's special usage of form. All that one glimpses is a final shot (semi-consciously); together with her Momma's dark head lowering and plus incandescent sulphur, as well as an opened egress point and her outstretched paw. Childishly, it dramatically pleas with fate's dealt hand!

X

Notwithstanding any of this, the family discovered that her body was too short for its casket. Now – when lifted by plenty of poverty in bereavement – they decided to tilt the girl's head to the leftside… somewhat radically and aplenty. This enabled a prior fit to be obtained with the coffer – in order to prevent one of Professor Gunter von Hagens' plastinates. Might it take root in terms of a grave's absence; or like Jeremy Bentham's auto-icon of yesteryear? Because, in a way reminiscent of third worlders all over, this clan supported a general ignorance; leastwise once their daughter had experienced the hot earth. For the buried cannot shake the land; especially given their interment beneath it!

XI

Still though – in our alternative reality – the blue skin stands provocatively on a roof-top or a neighbouring incline. Her boots are splayed or turned inwards; while her purple girdle curls instinctively this way and that over her scarcely concealed vagina. Behind her a hardly noticeable male assistant seeks cover in the wind. He wears a violently red tie. About her sphinx-like head the clouds scuttle and this is before our naked android makes her way back into the building's shelter – after Fritz Lang's capers. It was not easy being an icon, you know (?)... always open to others' expectations and thence becoming an instrument for their yearning. (Isn't this the name of the Ba'thist secret police in various mid-east states?) Statuesquely then, she turns and walks towards an empty elevator... whilst the dear-man waits for her in his cubicle. He remains obedient to a higher purpose thereby. It must be difficult resembling a torch which flickers in darkness, so as to lead the masses or *canaille* into a lucid awakening. Most abrasively or in conclusion, A.R. Orage's notion of the new age has become increasingly ancient by now.

XII

All of a sudden a darksome shape began to appear on moonlit nights or gloomy travails... It curved against our witches' sister with her head held unnaturally – or cast down in a leftwards direction. Do you see? Certainly, those who beheld her within deep vegetation of a maximum greenness sought to run hollering to the Gods! Oh yes... For Voodoo had been suspected over the youngster's demise – especially given the Houngan's infatuation. Her form was now a twilight shambler and it linked up with George Romero's spawn (thereby), or it betokened a zombie. This mulatto has now become one of Haiti's itinerants or walking dead; with her blood-shot eyes averted... or themselves rheumy and virtually pupilless (most drear). Each orb then remained at the socket's top or pinnacle; while staring vertically aslant or abreast of a Y-axis. Since wasn't there an occasion where a stretched limo burst through a roadblock – multi-dimensionally speaking? It caromed into a doorway and shattered the wooden fastness therein. Whereupon our Venus- blue ducked down and ran for such an aperture. A humanoid stag stood over her all this time and fired at assailants who can't be seen. (Note: surely these dream sequences are a record of the girl's status as a zombie... once the black magician's spell has taken effect?)

XIII

Given these events, then, even Papa Doc's delinquent authority acted in order to expel the Houngan from his territory. He went when surrounded by armed police and shackled to each officer by means of multiple bracelets. Everyone of this island's myrmidons eyed him uneasily – and weren't they really just examples of the Tonton Macoutes or the militia through which 'Papa' ruled? A self-confessed believer in Voodoo, Francois Duvalier had the mage banished --- but not prosecuted. He left spitting and cursing imprecations at all and sundry... only possibly to end up in the capital known as Port-au-Prince.

XIV

Meanwhile, a girl with a flash down her face woke up screaming or agog. She has been experiencing a recurrent nightmare, (you see); and this involves a phantasm which features her mother's desertion over and over again. May the cell door to this compound have been left open in order for them to make their escape? On the way out a reduced version of Enid Blyton's *troupe* – which consists of a fawn and her pet bear – look back. What do they notice? Why, it is little more than a cobalt matriarch who was stood in front of a computer-bank or a wall of television sets – while eyeing up her odds. In an instant a daughter and a Paddington toy are out of there. For whatever did Albert Camus say about freedom (?); namely, it happened to be a decreasing feeling of exhilaration a mere half-hour after release!

XV

The Houngan's victim, however, never made a full recovery and she lived out her remaindered days within her own community. But – from dawn to dusk – she didn't tell tales and linguistic inarticulateness loomed over all. Nor would her betrothed or engagement party wish to resurface. Who wants to marry a zombie… in consequence? Whilst, from the first to the last day, her cranium was badly skewed throughout this ordeal; the latter being a testament to her time under a coffin's lid. *Rest in Peace… for the dead wake angrily.*

THE END

SIXTY-FOOT DOLLS
a scientific romance

A switch, a moon and a wee 'bonnie' loon... *och-aieee* --- Old Scotch rime

ONE

A grill behind the bed served as an exit; or was it possibly a trellis-work beyond one's brain? Adjacent to which a large pillow propped up an aged head; the former being a severance or a grey dome that lilted towards black-current in terms of its hair dye. An orange blanket lowered down its frame and it waxed complacent *avaunt* a balustrade. Is it made of metal at our bed's end? Most definitely, a side-table existed in all its starkness and it stood next to this couch with a large pewter jug situated on its middle. A glass, at once holding a tooth-brush inside it, lay in close proximity. Further afield various rectangles intruded and they patched up to some light green... thence indicating a rhombus before folding back on themselves. Surely a yellow square of window subsisted outside or beyond our ken? Likewise, the proportions or perspectives of this agency indicated a picture. (Possibly one of William Nicholson's spare landscapes comes to mind... and can't he be remembered as slightly more than Ben's father?)

\+

A few nurses talked on in conclave and next to egress' happenstance. Whilst – somewhat alternatively – an aged patient lay in his bed over the way. A dullish, off-grey lampshade coalesced next to his wizened head and it appeared to kindle a 'fifties design.

\+

In the room's centre stood two doctors who were both dressed in their customary white coats. One indicated a younger age; while the other illustrated a stoic spore or Seneca's likeness to Nero's indulgence. Their names were Pickford and Carruthers-Smythe, and delicately placed black ties refused to distinguish them...

(Although one wore a crisp white offering; whilst his companion resounded to a pink gesture). Yes... Carruthers-Smythe demarcated the older man with Pickford tail-gunning for youth. (If we may speak of the two of them inhabiting an imaginary bi-plane – even one of a Great War vintage). A balding gloss oversmeared Smythe's head – plus NHS spectacles to match. Whereas his younger colleague towed a black circumference... at once wrapped around the skull after some hair's thrift. Both of them had stopped before one bed and it housed the oldest Chelsea pensioner in existence. His name was Adam.

TWO

Adam's inner processes are confounded one from another – and yet they do occur. None can look into his brain's recesses anymore... so aged is the individual who's served up to our analysis at this time. But deep within the cerebral cortex various memories stir and neurone circuits are activated thereby. They whiz, pop, crackle and startle roundabouts... all of it leading to variously fresh projects. Or – in truth – does Adam reach back to visions so ancient that they come out fresh... no matter how indelicately? Anyway, within a memory-bank such as this the following mesmerisms subsist. It basically betokens a new grace's fixture – only then to reveal a green sky lit by lightening flashes. A large fortress – consisting of dull brick – exists outside one particular time-zone. Oughtn't this century really to be many years ahead or maybe on another world? Improvidently, such a structure existed on New Britain *circa.* 3421 and it rested on the western edge of Crowthorne, a town in Berkshire's royal county. Once upon a time it had been called Broadmoor and it lay either obscured or whitened out on sundry ordinance survey maps. Mightn't it have been a hospital for what Lombroso, Galton, Stekel, Krafft-Ebing and even Weininger called the criminally insane? Still, one has to recall Gaius Cibber's statues to 'Melancholy' and 'Raving Madness' here... namely, these were the ones which manifested themselves on Bedlam's walks. Weren't they the reversal – morally speaking – of the *Art Brut* that was housed in the Maudsley hospital, south London? Essentially though, currents of solid brick lay about such a tone... what with some plate windows very high up and made of lead. While earth tremors hampered this bivouac roundabout or adjacent to it, and each blast caused the ground's vicinity to break up!

THREE

Doctor Pickford has invented a serum which not only reduces ageing but that reverses its effects... by the by. Wonder of wonders! Now then, he's come to Magdalene's Mercy Seat in order to test it out – if we are to steal a line from Samuel Beckett. Whereas Carruthers-Smythe, a lower order doctor in this food queue, is merely the chief orderly at such a hospice. Moreover, why don't they throw all caution to the winds by using our dormitory's oldest patient as a guinea pig? To be sure: Adam lies almost preternaturally withered in a bed or curled up with age. He is wrinkled, gnarled, escape-free and without any vacuous intent. Also, his burden lies before death --- somewhat exquisitely --- and in a manner that Heidegger would have approved of in terms of *Dasein*. The top-sheet virtually touches his chin or pout, with a texture which was creamy-to-white and remained somehow off-blue. Again, his skin flays a brillo pad's palimpsest; whilst it stays haltered to grey and even fibrous in its drift. How – one asks – can a scarecrow like this be brought back onto life's continent? Yet assuredly, Doctor Pickford illumines the way onto a *terra incognita*. For – like Merlin – he doesn't doubt his countenance or ready abacus; at least in terms of Herman Hesse's glass beads. Nor does he discount the vagaries of fate or a similar happenstance. After all, Adam has lain on a cot longer than most orderlies can recall. It was as if his truckle-bed imprisons him... whereupon days drift by in terms of hours, minutes or months. Let's face it, then: these two medicine men overlook him and analyse success' arch... particularly when limned in blue.

FOUR

On Adam's cerebral cortex another drama unfolds its banner. Without doubt, it has no need for a bookish theatrical agency and embodies Nick Hern Books thereby. Especially when this deals with Peter Nichols' 'seventies diaries or Caryl Churchill's demotic translation of Seneca's *Thyestes* – itself raw from the Latin and by way of Atreus' fall. Do your crystals register such a livery? For within these corridors of power a female android makes her rounds. A grey pall of steel sweeps away behind her visage and it's merely registered over undelivery… as she carries a residue of drinks on a silver tray. It glistens in artificial light or splendour – while on its surface a pitcher of light-red liquid spills. Two tumblers remain adjacent to its absent pollution… or isn't that some residual polish? Regardless of this: her name sports a twin with Andalusia and she's about six-feet tall. Highly erotic whilst remaining antiseptic – she had magenta garters of a refined plastic which come up to her thighs… In a situation where her overall body waxes green; and thus spreads out with a lost translucence or sheen. Further, a coif of blonde hair that is basically modelled short curves delicately across her forehead. Wherein the perfectly proportioned body supports globular breasts which rest on a reclining wave… with various fixtures and fittings aft. Does one see now? It all relates to these cylindrical tendencies of *eros* that hone in on G-spots or erogenous zones… when each one can be traced by its extremities. They effectively take up a format of long-evolved ear-rings. May they betoken a reptilian state of consciousness in accord with three-brain theory: as explicated by Arthur Koestler in *Bricks to Babel*? Likewise, serpentine arm-cords pitch up near a right shoulder or its ambit; and these connect with wrist bracelets and shine with dulled gold… somewhat ambidextrously. Do they indicate an 18-carat Magnificat? To be sure: a golden bodice wraps around her torso and it just links to one movement; and it extends from a cupped mammary all the way round to her crotch… itself aswirl. Are we then left with geometrical eyes, lips and brows…? For this goddess' mouth glistens with plastic resin: whereas the nymph's eye-brows arch after Marlene Dietrich. Could she be a *green* as against Pabst's *Blue* Angel?

FIVE

The doctor's face limbered up towards Adam's profile in this geriatric ward. In these circumstances – then – both of them were virtually sat on a truckle bed's edge. Doctor Pickford stared wide-eyed (you see); with one azure orb revolving in its socket aslant of a bristling brow. Also, a blue swathe cut about the doc's tunic or surplice – when essentially risking ought else but a sallow indifference. This oldster who was named after the Old Testament's original man held his ground… even though a crepuscular hand did play about his lips. Irrespective of which – Adam's flesh-tone came out grey and it almost rusted to iron, so corrosive did these flakes of metal seem when hidden from his intent. None of Robert Aickman's ghouls blustered anymore now! For Methuselah looked on and stared at Pickford square in the face. Truly, Dorian Gray's portrait has freed itself from the flame; only to then be rather repositioned (hectoringly) in a mirror. Must we pursue an analysis herein (?); particularly given Rene Magritte's painting concerning a 'stopped reproduction'. Nonetheless, any real identikit relates to Edgar Allan Poe's story *The Tell-Tale Heart*. Wherein a madman's eye turns a corner in a distended fashion and thereby looks on – rather like Odin's glass which became detached from its retina after a bout on the world's tree. How can we take any proper bearings? Since Adam's prism rediscovers a light-source: while it stares on like a marble whose sluice mechanism finds itself tilted sideways. Did it embody a Victorian doll in this regard? Any road up, Adam has most certainly received the Queen's telegram… thence indicating a vintage due to age and prior to wine's humiliation. Hadn't either of them come across the allegory *Mister Weston's Good Wine* by T. F. Powys? Yesss… To be certain of it, this centenarian's mop doused some grey hemp or a curlicue of wool: the latter busily redeeming baldness.

+

"Don't you want to be young again, Adam?", enquired Doctor Pickford. He seemed to be genuinely in earnest – as if mounting an evangelical crusade or mission. Surely no-one in their right mind could reject such an *elixir vitae*? "Just a little injection", posited our white jacket, "and you'll be able to insure a lost life. Maybe you wish to walk abreast of our sun (?); or possibly find the full effulgence of its rays once more? Think man, you can step out of a body that's raddled with disease and into the *corpus* of an Apollo… or even a Dionysus minus his cups. Wouldn't you exchange a male crone for the life of Macbeth's saviour…? Truly, a double-take may be yours at this juncture. Exchange Scrooge's lineaments for Myron's *Discobolos*, I beg you! Make the break… senilitics of the world unite; you have nothing to lose but your colostomy bags!" "I reject youth", hissed our elder berry. "'T'is time's fool; it will not endure --- please let's praise its absence. Like Sir Oswald Mosley's work *The Alternative* after the war, I prefer to dream along dissimilar lines. May one notice it aright? There are too many responsibilities in being young, you see. Each to his own… I am content with oblivion or even brain liquefaction. Do you remember the emperor Claudius (?); why yes… for the Praetorians insisted on making him *imperator* after Caligula's assassination. But he may not have really required it… A quiet life is what furnishes sleep; albeit with no lisping there, nor epilepsy and a wish of ages. Who would have married Messalina had they enjoyed the truth (?) – whether one reads either Robert Graves or Albert Jarry for a choice of partner. No – young divine – I refuse your bait and no hamsters are waiting here for life's chop. My frame's lived too great a time already and I can't bear the spectrum all over again – not even counting up every sun-dial's requiem. It is an endless return without any stay of execution. I refuse your wonder drug's jab or MMR vaccine… do ya hear?" His voice trailed away like a mouse caught in its trap with a screech. There was no echo hereabout and no cheese to speak of.

SIX

Andalusia hummed to herself while walking along. (Even though these events took place in Adam's recesses… and perhaps he wished to draw his bus pass in order to savour them more?) Instead of which she gambolled with fate's stray partiality… nonetheless. For what looks like a weapon gathers pace behind her and it shines out of a deep patch of darkness – irrespective of any sheen. Our robot, though, bends down her beautiful head so as to arrange one's drinks. They stir restively in their liquidity – particularly as she swirls them with a see-through glass pole. Her blonde coif hangs over abreast of a blue forehead; while the girl's heavy ear-rings slant across towards a Bishop's diagonal. Our green android's lips are pursed; and this was despite her inner locution or timbre. An unseen presence – by the by – acknowledges her want of care. Truly, it begins now…

SEVEN

"Hey, slow down in your affidavit's travesty", burbled Doctor Pickford. "No-one wishes to force you down a lane you don't want to travel on. No sir… please remember (also) that we dispute the theories of Jack Kevorkian and Peter Singer. We still imbibe the Hippocratic Oath in this practice, you know? When doctors like ourselves recognise the illicit nature of compulsion, if it's used to entice you into a snake's mouth. By the way, do you recognise Richard Westmacott the Elder's monument to James Dutton in Sherborne, Gloucestershire *circa*. 1791. It transfigures a guardian angel standing above a sacrificial urn with its arms aloft and wings outstretched. Presumably, she's releasing Dutton's corse or skeleton so as to permit its ascent… at least in accord with Christian notions over bodily resurrection, physically speaking. Why man, I'm able to offer you a similar route without any deviousness! A pinch of my serum and the years will fall away like a snake's shed skin. One final point, Adam, seeing your reluctance to speculate… how old are you?"

+

Old father time stopped to consider – somewhat ruminatively. "A consequence of these days misses my sun-dial thereafter. No topiary over such a bracken's need can really stick in the flesh. For our pericarp happens to be a rind concerning Zeus' *ennui*… after all. Don't manufacture a moment of mayhem on my account, I beg you. Yet I do recall the odd jibe from way back in the past… To illustrate it better, what about a peeling of bells at the Boer War's end around 1902?" As he remarks this the oldster's skin limps towards a grey or taut aspect; and it's almost like the wire in one of Angus Calder's mobiles. Or – more accurately – may it intone those thin, elongated structures of Giacometti (?); and this is never mind those images of Jean Genet *et al.* Weren't they even more etiolated, whey-faced, desperate and anaemic than usual? Undoubtedly, it came to register John Tyndall's strictures in *The Eleventh Hour*… especially when his analysis undermines a tension in today's polity (*anno humanae salutis*). While he compared the body politic to an AIDS victim; i.e., a breeding ground which lacks immunity's infection. During this period, though, Adam's eyes glowed preternaturally like coals in their sockets… all of it amid some ashen surroundings. Needless to say, this proved to be no matter how cavernously he was taken off… and didn't he embody a shrunken Jerzy Kosinski in milk?

EIGHT

As of this moment – however – Andalusia has yet to open her orbs. For a sparkle of light lit up the gun's outer circle or cusp; and it refracted from its prism (thereby). It came out of blackness' square quadrant or rectangle; and was at once limited to a camera's dexterity. Seemingly then, our robot's light blue and blonde head remained undisturbed. Moreover, we notice that her eyes are closed, tranquil and almost stoical without any residual faith. She continues to alter her drinks' equilibrium throughout. What does this version of the robot woman in Fritz Lang's *Metropolis* hum to herself? "Love", she sings, "love remains --- only to be --- by celebrity --- a way to break free… or a malady". Certainly, *mon amour*, yet the numinous behind her generates a shadow or an opal's power. It thinks resultantly within a spore's contagion (in other words). Such synapses postulate the following: "no longer will I face ridicule by being marginalised over a pupil's point – let alone when loosened within Calvin's *Institutio*. No. The master must make certain of his gold before such an entrapment. This I swear --- by dint of any intrigue!" Such a girl-toy has a destiny to fulfill which proves to be irrespective of any other function. May she be reborn cybernetically (?); if only to rise like a phoenix within Dennis Wheatley's *The Satanist*. You see, Spenser's *Faery Queen* has nothing on this conundrum: it posits death – somewhat inescapably in a God's ash-bowl – and circumnavigates a dish while wriggling after an asp. Don't the serpent-folk indicate knowledge in the West's pantheon?

NINE

Doctor Pickford has turned his back on a patient's rudeness – yet he still speaks to himself. "Why, it's incredible, Carruthers-Smythe, now I come to think of it. Yonder fellow believes he was here at Vereeniging's peace (in 1902) when the Afrikaners sued for armistice with the British empire! That's unbelievable, my assistant, and it means our oldster's at least a century plus four years of age… Do you exemplify Weston's monument to Jonathan and Elisabeth Ivie in St. Petrock's church, Exeter, around 1717? An understanding of this is brought to my mind – whether severally or against one's grain. At least, however, such a bass-relief signals a last judgement or paean, after a preliminary which shoots forwards towards William Blake. Whereupon two skulls look out and guard the flanks; in a scenario where both of them appear to be reclining on a severance of leaves… Isn't Adam really a refutation of the body's resurrection (to be sure)? Surely on his crust we note that cremation would make the better sense (?); i.e., merely by leaving such droplets to form a foot-guard on the curb". "Forget him", admonishes Carruthers-Smythe rather brusquely. "Our records are extensive and somewhat over-indulged. For truly, we practice what we preach in a drama where Max Weber's critique of bureaucracy holds sway. We definitely believe in the iron cage *tout court*. Come across the way, Doctor Pickford, and consult our filing cabinets in a rival bureau. This office, like Kafka's insurance one dealing with Prague's claims, rectifies all lies. Given the circumstances, no mendacity escapes from such a limited filo-fax. Let's play it by numbers, Doctor Pickford, since Adam's true age will stand revealed on his outermost envelope. Check it out, colleague, but I'm convinced that he's ageless in death's face!"

TEN

Now proved to be the moment where Andalusia noticed aught amiss… For she felt a presence behind her in the ether, somewhat inquisitively. The gun to one side of her is discernible now – it just points out from a tomb's dark sanctum. It illuminates a black cube; thereby floating in its ebon void or geometry… and silencing all critics. In a subdued glow's light – the robot's skin passes a luminous sweetness or pelt; possibly indicating a latex's shine in terms of its composition. Her eye remains closed; while the lightening flash above it almost intones a Mosleyite arrow… albeit when traversing a parallel beam. Does she continue to sing? Most definitely, in a troubadour's vein she warbles: "Love waxes a sin --- chief of all Djinn --- and routed to win --- by dint of a limb, all credit to spin. Yesss…" Yet may such considerations be overmastered and unburdened, or even subsumed, by philosophy's back-turn? Also, the rival mind beyond her continues in spate: "Our girl-toy silences insouciance's bride, but I won't take the indifference of this curtailment. No: since my master seeks to avoid such registered squares as these. In any event, this mosaic's confection fails to alter its stroboscopic glow or tint. Nor can it be dismissed as Victor Pasmore's patterning, as concerns the cover of J.P. Stern's *Nietzsche* in Fontana's modern patchwork. Do you see? What began life – aesthetically speaking – as a protest against bourgeois society has ended up as wall-paper. Because corporate capitalism uses *The Painted Word* – to adopt Tom Wolfe's satire – as an emptying of standard content or a spectacle of visual consumption. It all goes to delimit Ortega Y Gasset's thesis, in his *The Dehumanisation of Art*, that modernism rejects humanism in apotheosis. Didn't the central intelligence agency (CIA) back abstract expressionism in *Encounter* magazine during the 'sixties?" But Andalusia has heard something; it cracks a floor-tile aslant her.

ELEVEN

Doctor Pickford stoops to examine each elevation in turn. In this instance, he stands amid a collection of metallic cases. They are wedged up against a wall in a dun-coloured office; the lino-cut of which is off-green. To begin with he's slightly bored or dulled, and our doc thumbs through the attendance records casually. Nothing breaks his calm throughout this procedure. Yet suddenly, he becomes incredulous. "What about it, eh? This tabulation goes back further and further… albeit with every notice relying on improvidence. The dates fly past one: merely being a logarithm that skims in posterity's face or breeds exponentially. (Albeit reverse-wise, for here in this time-tunnel the years proceed over a boundary's horizon). First off, he's recollected as being around in 1974 – i.e., in close proximity to Harold Wilson's tired election. But behold: then comes 1950 – during a period where Labour's landslide falls sheer. It was rather like a portrait of the dissident Irish writer Francis Stuart – when put on canvas by Jack Crabtree. You know, he's the one who broadcast to Hibernia on Axis radio? The face looks rather wiry, sunken, melancholic and capable of renewed life… even if set deeply in repose. Certainly, it exemplifies the Gael's skeletal embrace – essentially after an impasto or the thick paint of Jack B. Yeats. Doctor Pickford decides to delve further afield. He turns – with renewed gusto – to a rival filing cabinet.

TWELVE

Each twilight spelt out its foretold vampirism once more. For now the shape which menaces Andalusia took a physical form… even a three-dimensional eddy. Didn't it realise, *en passant*, a misprisionment or a blob – the like of this standing with a pistol in its mouth? Or so she wished… Summarily, a bank of machinery became discernible behind her. It whistled towards grey or a pumice's tone; primarily in terms of a lost tournament. During this the boom-tube's red mouth leapt into prominence or exhibited itself. Our robot has fallen silent now and no ditties, worthy of Arne or Purcell, trip from her synthetic lips. Whilst her eye – surrounded by fibrous eye-lashes – had opened wide in the interval. Its most suggestive feature is a negative pupil; because within one's socket no eye-ball manifests itself… there was merely the solace of an empty plexi-glass sliver. To be fair, a throaty if sibilant voice calls out: "Yo-ho, beauteous one! Oh, Andalusia?"

+

Whereupon the weapon's safety catch clicks onto a FIRING POSITION.

THIRTEEN

Doctor Pickford's head turns narrowly over its shoulder's impress. A dull-looking filing cabinet – replete with papers – leads away from his gaze. He also holds a yellowing manuscript in his hand. "It can't be borne, Carruthers-Smythe…", yelps our investigator. "Since such a *pabulum* confirms that our ancient mariner has been here since the Anglo-Boer war's end. Never mind Thomas Pakenham; let's consider Sir Arthur Conan Doyle's 'Official History' of the conflict. Adam must have occupied yonder truckle-bed (or one like it) for a hundred-and-four years. Come on…" But his medical orderly remains stoical throughout this. "Our home's records never resort to disorder, sir", he purrs. "Why not consult these treatment papers lying roundabout? Truly, facts emerge from ancient newsprint; it reflects algebra's needs. More than likely, though, it will prove to be Marc Quinn's blood mask in terms of its efficacy (presumably). Don't you reminisce about his Turner Prize exhibit (?); namely, the one kept alive or pursuant to its Kelvin temperature. It betokens congealed *Dasein* and evidences the fragility of Keats' death-mask… as taken by an Italian sculptor. My thumb folds over one discoloured sheet, but Quinn unmasks the *self* so as to foster cunning. What could be more natural, after all, than death's wanton semblance? Does refrigeration keep it alive, alive-o?"

FOURTEEN

The blast from an atomic gun cast off to her veriest roots – thus causing Andalusia to 'die'! Even though robots cannot really perish; they only await re-programming or replenishment at a later time. To be sure: the ray cut through her machinery almost erotically or viscerally, and *in lieu* of its penetration. The beauteous robot screamed aloud with her mouth an olive template – only to then rebound before a green sounding-board. Her limbs – at once gauntleted to a measure – were flung out and back, and the blonde head almost threw itself sideways. Maybe it was in transport or livid to *coitus*, even? Still, our manufactured grave saw her breasts ruptured or crepitating with false ardour; and they are bifurcated to a reed. Might it be considered a supermodel's revenge on her robotic other? Seemingly, the thighs happen to be open and convulsed in this *demarche*… while their roundness waxed cylindrical after Raquel Welch's fashion. Each leg bifurcates towards purple now – just tearing magenta down and by way of two pins' proportioned curves.

FIFTEEN

Whereas Carruthers-Smythe – Doctor Pickford's apologist – stared with growing disbelief at a sovran bit of paper. Yellow it was; whilst owning up to a previous existence… Surely it happened to be those commitment papers – merely tattered by awe and lore – which spoke of Adam's entrance to the hospital many moons before? The date concerned (when read cautiously) is Wednesday the twelfth 1902. Confound this conclusion… for in light of it Smythe's mind knows both mugg and confusion. A mist or a delimited ether descends thereafter. Could it be nitrous oxide or laughing gas – if taken mistakenly? Carruthers rubbed his fingers over his nose's bridge… a possible reflex (this) or the beginnings of an alienist's case-study? Wide-eyed, he re-addressed himself to the sheet or its chlorine's whiteness. He held its remnants betwixt thumb and forefinger. "Doctor, our institution's records remain second to none. In truth, nothing can be dismissed as belonging to a pluperfect tense (no matter how arbitrarily). This screed merely states: "Adam Bartholomew Jefferson (sic) gained admission to this hospice in ---- . He has two conspicuous birthmarks picked out on his upper back. By the way, his twin or later names – Bartholomew and Jefferson – were our staff's attributions. The individual was an aged tramp who went only by Adam's suffix. Already – and at this early stage – he proved to be showing *senility's advanced creep*."

+

Also – while making these remarks – a sudden image came into Carruthers-Smythe's lobes. It resembled a multi-faceted serpent which looks long and globular – with a sea of porous cells sapping away beneath it. Each waxed to a vaguely testicular curvature or promontory; itself amid a pendulous ooze of red and green DNA. Suffice it to say, then, they had about them something of the cancers that afflicted Professor R.A. Willis' *The Pathology of Tumours* published by Butterworths in 1942. Out of which a worm ouroboros slowly emerged. Susceptibly, it might be the snake that devours its tail down many contours or intrigues, and while devouring each swish. No. For here it merely rose up when driven by light and pale turquoise in its fillet: whilst posturing to a grave. Various tentacles then salaamed in the nether distance and were now suffused with a tunnel's azure… whilst crepitating in the dawn under a haloed planet. The creature's eyes wept blankly or vacantly, and are seemingly suffused to a skin's parchment (thereby). Whereupon its maw superintended over all… an orifice (this) which came up open, raw, limpid, 'Blimp', comatose and even retching to oblivion! It was surrounded by canines around an orifice that gapes – rather like an early surrealist magazine called *Minotaur*. Much of this conjures up a screaming Pope – after Velasquez's example – and by Francis Bacon. Here though, it betokened a meat-grinder instead of Freud's castration complex… even if its teeth cheated T-Rex. While 'it' cleaved to a free continent; at once lost in gore and open to bile by implication. Didn't this elemental's dehiscence ramble forth like an ice worm?

+

No sooner had he conjured up this image than Carruthers-Smythe promptly forgot it.

SIXTEEN

Doctor Pickford returned swiftly to Adam's bed-side. He looked down on him loftily and from higher up. How dare you(!), he thought *apropos* of nothing in particular. But he let it slide with some sort of contrivance. "Adam, tell me this", he said – as he resorted to Samuel Richardson's rhetoric. "How far back do you recall historical junctures, eh?" "I don't know", mumbled Adam in contrast, "leave me alone." Yet Doc Pickford's scientific curiosity was pricked now! Even though the bed-stead looked off-white as before… when sat next to a sickly green wall. A pigment --- this --- which betrayed all sense of optimism. Despite these features, though, Adam looked sprightly and completely in charge of his faculties… somewhat surprisingly. Where is our crematoria's urn(?); and this is irrespective of the great age or sarcophagus mongering that burdened him.

SEVENTEEN

Speaking of mortality – however – the 'form' which wielded a gun became discernible now. Perhaps it was a split formulation (?); being basically relevant to Adam but otherwise distinct. It may be Andalusia's *animus* in Jung's sliver; as misdirected or seen from without and thus "incarnate". Anyway, Adam II was obese with a stretched jerkin down to his knees – rather like a peon in *Ivanhoe*. His feet pop out on stubby legs from what appears to be a mediaeval smock (primarily). Likewise, can it address a calling that reverberates to Georg Baselitz's name; albeit with his reverse paintings in mind? Upside-down they are; plus Baselitz's paint is drip-fed into an unknowing tube. Does one really care? Also, some of the publications *avec* these on their covers include William S. Burroughs' *Queer* and *Junky* – both of which are early works. Nonetheless, Adam II's forearm and face are uncovered; and each waxes muscular to its defeat by being necessarily monstrous or otherwise inflated. It comes after a recognition of Lewis Caroll's Humpty-Dumpty or egg; a character who, post-structurally, believed that words can be made to mean what you like. Adam II also has a succulent orb under an eye-lid; the latter merely hatched to a brilliant white. While the hair which exists atop one's mask remains thatched, Brillo-like, Hecate inducing or liable to make over Macbeth's three sisters… out of Fuseli's example. These features rather memorably signify Fat: whether it be rolling, flabby, multi-dimensional, pummelled, hanging, dough-like or coruscated. His livery – irrespective of a ray-gun in its mitten – then notices both emerald, dice and ebon.

EIGHTEEN

Meanwhile, Doctor Pickford has acted on his curiosity. Had he fallen prey to what Moreau – the vivisector in H.G. Wells' romance – once called the "colourlessness of pure research"? To be quick about it: our centenarian has been led naked into the examining room. May all of this quicken an Adamite pulse? Oh yes… since the fluoroscope's eerie glow flickers into life resultantly. Both Carruthers-Smythe and Pickford study the oldster intently. They looked at his body – whether quickened to a spasm or not – and seen through a fluorescent screen. Likewise, this glass-box represents a fish-tank most rare – what with Adam's grey mop bobbing up and down above its Rediffusion list. Pickford's and Carruthers-Smythe's faces or profiles then looked on at an amazing hinterland… all of it unknown to medical science. The younger white coat stares particularly in disbelief. His head appears above and slightly to the side of its colleague. Moreover, their features are illumined in a ribena's tint – all of it linked to a shifting ultramarine. It pulsates – stroboscopically – within a Roentgen ray's glow; while kaleidoscope's shimmer from one spectrum's end to another inside a darkened room. Didn't Newton experiment in Cambridge with refractions via prisms (?); and by way of holes bored in blinds. Every world turns full circle, you see? "It is impossible", expostulated our Pickford. "A trick has been perpetrated on Gray's *Anatomy*. Look here – some hoaxer must have become lost at his work bench. I refuse to countenance such stud poker. Not even a sculptor like Brancusi can carve a minimal head from the Cyclades like this… especially on its side. Do you hear?" His older assistant keeps shushed throughout… because there was an hysterical hint in Pickford's voice.

NINETEEN

Against such grains – though – Andalusia's robotic head is spied from one side. Seen in profile it may well be: with after-care's necessary lost witness and despite any provenance such as this. For her lambent skin glows in the dark or gloom, and it possesses a limpid extraction of emerald in its undulating contrasts. Could it reconnoitre a stanley knife, thereby? Or, more truthfully, does it absolve any other transformation --- moving, as I say, from turquoise to pthalo by way of permanent green. All before it morphs into a lighter gesture still… isn't it then really abreast of Hooker's green? Whilst an abundance of sap and citrus – when out of chromium oxide and olive – threw itself onto photosynthesis' screen. Still, the blanched sockets are without wit and her blonde coif remains active… albeit all around the scalp. Heavy ear-rings lay adjacent to her grassy calm; they were tabulated in ormolu. Whereas her mouth looked like a cherub's orb and it resiled to a cry's opening gesture… as it evinces or occasions a steamy evaporation. It recoils like a serpent *in lieu* of any taste – but no Stygian interlude can hide its eroticism. In this instance, it records a gloss on Felicien Rops' painting of a *danse macabre*. A smearing of liquid – at once boiling up to pearlescence – runs down her cheek's side. "Absence of self-repair", murmurs her internal or cybernetic system. Surely it happens to be in the process of shutting down?

+

Behind her, however, a wall of grey hides its oblivion. It sequesters into shapes or various squares… all of which are beholden to many colours. Furthermore, the tray of drinks and snacks – itself recalling astronaut's food – slips across a parquet flooring out of bounds.

TWENTY

"Look", said Doctor Pickford with asperity, "this man hasn't got a heart. Observe, Carruthers-Smythe, do you make out where my finger-tip points?" To this end, his pink mitten gestured at a fluorescent screen beyond. It waxed on jasper or let out a refrain which bore upon some X-rays. Certainly – within this mock-television or cathode ray oscilloscope – a vertebrate's longing stood out. It curved up like an insect's mandible gesture; if only to elongate nature's fractures. In this it realised nought else… since various grey dials were prominent next to one's glass. Incidentally, a pelvis reared up and filleted a lower retinue, or was otherwise caged to its necessity. Although Professor Gunter von Hagens' plastinates brooked no complaint here… because Vesalius' tissue snorted at Gray's efforts. Further – our troubadour listed to one side; and this is almost like a centipede or a millipede. Again, such a puppeteer has been flayed or faced the rhythm of a threshing instrument. But throughout this ordeal it is noticeable that Adam kept silent. No article of speech passed his lips. Carruthers-Smythe, the assistant, also mimed along to Pan's pipe.

+

What could 'Doc' Pickford essay, though? Really, it went after such participles as these… since his mind became convulsed with a stray thought. During which interlude a serpentine worm doubled back on its carcass. A blade had shorn the head from its body – thence leaving its trunk to writhe on the ground in controlled contortions. Still and all, these palpitations stroked a cellular tomb or they manifested a yellow claw that groped feverishly. One sallow head popped up with jaded gems for eyes or slits, and it was somewhat gloomily witnessed. Throughout this a naked damsel with snakes around each breast danced the tarantella. She did so in the background near a nethermost crypt. Our young Pickford only entertained this phantasm momentarily, however… thus dismissing it.

TWENTY-ONE

Andalusia's body will have been carried away by her assailant now. The shape which has done so can be seen from behind (forsooth). It stands out against several rectangular barricades – all of them illustrating opal when awash with pumice. Let's see: her mouth – entertaining Asimov's vision of not *I Robot* – continues to smoke. Perhaps a brackish incense poured out that was unknown to Heaven's redundance? Her purple bootlegs also swung obligingly --- when next to Adam's right arm. Yet, intra-dimensionally, it is Adam who's making off with some booty… itself merely replete to a capture. No murmur can be heard. All one recognises happens to be its bulk – as limned in a corridor or gesturally observed. Essentially though, Adam seems well pleased with his work… for hasn't he imprisoned a female side or tic? After all – in pure Kabbalism – Lilith's sin is necessary… because she falls from life's tree only to redeem it, and in order to overcome dualism or provide ascent's possibility. Can't this unite duality's primal form beyond the provenance of man and woman, male or female? Yes indeed… let us forget the pseudo-Kabbala of Madonna and concentrate on G.G. Scholem's Jewish mysticism instead. Since Lilith can intrude even before Jehovah in legend. Wasn't her necessary evil spirituality's quanta; or the mechanics of a freedom to will? Or put another way – should assertive liberty betray its absence? Above all, as evidenced by *Genesis* Chapter Five; Verse Three, our night's demoness came to be Adam's first wife. Yet truthfully, are all of Asmodeus' children worthy of their mother?

TWENTY-TWO

Doctor Pickford grasped his head's back at this moment... almost in exasperation! Maybe it turned on a thyroid twitch (?); the likelihood of which led to an enervation – primarily of will. But no listlessness seized him. No – any prior atavism lay on another side altogether. He continued to stare in mystification at the fluoroscope. Adam lolled behind its wiles or loops – somewhat entranced. Moreover, his entire skeletal embrace – like the thirteenth tarot card signifying death – fell open before him. His rib-cage, salient bones, chattel and tooth-pick all stood revealed. Whilst across from this adventure (my friend) can't you detect an olive filament... no matter how lit up? Adam – our first or last man – grinned inanely over Roentgen's device... the nature of it delimited Galen. Hadn't he declared – even after vivisection – that a dog entertained two hearts which were both on the left? Further, this character's eyes are sunken or drifting, and thus indicate a by-law over such pits. Nor can we speak of blindness aslant these orbs, albeit in the manner of a pituitary cancer pressing on one's optic nerves. (This condition ultimately did for authors like John Milton or Wyndham Lewis – at least when blinding both afore letters' maturity). Didn't Lewis once declare in the face of a journalist's provocation that he had many books to write? Blindness stood as a plenitude to thraldom (therefore). "You insult me", he roared at this hack. "I'm unseeing not dead. One's lamp of aggressive voltage continues. I suffer from no want of power. The mind has many mansions." After this he constructed a modernist hell which was only fit to be witnessed from purgatory. It came superintended over by Sammael, a baroque prince of darkness. His publisher called it *Malign Fiesta.*

+

Several disc-like lights existed above Pickford while he spoke betimes. Whereupon Adam's lips – half above and below the scanner – looked like blue scallops… and each one was rubbery to the touch. Surely fate had meant something distinctive by this turn of events? Because Doctor Pickford's voice sounded uncertain throughout, rather than exasperated. "Will you examine those lungs, Carruthers-Smythe?", he asserted. "Entrance one's devils, man! I'd swear to it that they are not mortal. How can a humanoid breathe with yonder apparatus intact? It's almost as if they were constructed, *inter alia*, to inhale and exhale on another planet other than our earth." "Don't be absurd", expostulated his colleague. But he did so without force or conviction, and merely as an after-thought. Both of them have been captured or captivated (somewhat exhaustively) by this analog screen. What can it mean?

TWENTY-THREE

In our fellow dimension, though, Adam's *alter ego* surveys a dead nymph. Green she happens to be (perchance) and reminiscent of a *Playboy* centrefold in its ripe undulation! Her circumference is upended – albeit being reversed – and Andalusia lies head-first over a grey sledge. May it resemble a dais or an expectant moon's custodian? With any certitude her breasts are almost out – at least when contrasted with a gold bikini connected to a frame. A sore cleavage also reveals love's tunnel, basically insofar as this can be compared to the steam issuing roundabout. It susurrates a wound… while looking up forevermore. The green robot's blonde mop hangs down – if only to sacrifice a sort of ashen crucifixion in terms of Athene and Hephaistos creating Pandora, even Anesidora. Will not Andalusia incarnate a thousand starlets herein? Whether they were Jordan, Trine Michelson, Sarah Young, Caprice, Raquel Welch, Bo Derek, Pamela Anderson or Sylvia Krystal *et al.* Truly, and by way of reflexion, when does an *artiste* become a scarlet woman or what Marlene Dietrich called a *soldier of love*? Well, it surely hardly suffices with a robot! For Andalusia's mouth rests open in the form of a red opal plus some teeth, while next to this aperture a pale green rheum flowed freely. No-one knew its lost extent… whereas liquid from her inner circuitry has splashed on her breasts and thighs in what Lord Lichfield would call a *wet look.* Yet might the misshapen form above her, Adam, actually intend benevolence rather than its converse? His form luxuriates in Quasimodo's lustre (to be sure); yet who can say that he will be left alone with no-one to talk to after time's fullness? Since his ultimate intention was to give this *femme* his conscience – jurisprudentially speaking. He wants to reassemble her in order to reverse the usual trajectory of Adam and Eve. Now instead of the betrothed who bites into knowledge's apple at the behest of a serpent's wiles… we have Adam distressing Eve's purity through illumination. A second Lilith cannot emerge from such an egg, you see? In these circumstances, then, realism is the key to insight's ferocity. Didn't William S. Burroughs declare in a letter to Ginsberg that he was a factualist? He wished to return truth's maxim at every available level. So be it. This recycles or turns around the intentionality of Adam's self-regard. Suddenly he hears a BEEP-PEEP… the communication device! Master Pickford was obviously trying to contact him again. BEEP-PEEP.

TWENTY-FOUR

Our two physicians remain huddled before their fluoroscope – whereat everything in a circumambient mist turns green. Could it be some sort of portent? Moreover, the two of them became increasingly dumb-founded by today's evidence or slide-show. Now each of them crouched before olive celluloid or its plasma screen; together with a glassy surface of resin passing out amidships. To look at our scientists from behind – Carruthers-Smythe stooped slightly to one's left; while Doctor Pickford did spot-work from points right. A bank of cells, metallic note-pads, dials and rickety instruments collided with this reality… or lay to one side. Yes truly: thereupon it delivered a livery or a steel plate which recognised a ventriloquist's silver. Above all though, one luminance stood out beyond other matters. It was Adam's eyes. These gazed on like two lost orbs – both of them greenish and with their pupils highly dilated. To say that they represented a lost soul seems mawkish, even inconsiderate in its romanticism. Yet something of this sort came to pass. "What goes on here?", trilled Carruthers-Smythe. "Do you follow my reasoning? There's no discernible heart, radically abnormal lungs and the geriatric's over a century-and-a-half old... how is it to be explained?" For an instant his companion remained silent or rock-like. Then he spoke up by return of post. "There's only one possible opinion, Carruthers. We've got to operate on the oldster. By using my youth serum we'll force him backwards through reverse evolution and towards his mother's cervix, relatively speaking." "But isn't that unethical?", replied his companion. "Haven't we both heard him say why he doesn't wish to receive it...? Our controlling medical board may not be happy at *force majeure* – no matter one's object or purport." "Fiddle-sticks!", ejaculated Pickford with asperity. "Do you call yourself some sort of weakling, old boy? Let us press on remorselessly in the direction of pathology's dexterity or rind, as well as the innermost latitude of one's hidden matter. No-one calls a halt to it – just plunge in the knife abreast of a withering asp and its sores! Don't stay this blade's execution – we must be frank about it like a Robin Cook medical thriller. Didn't John Keats – before he became totally taken with his muse – always know that surgery began with a butcher's relief? Yessir. Append your name to these release papers, I beg you. Indulge me. No, nooo... I refuse to entreat, I demand it in science's name! As Professor Fred Hoyle remarks, we must make a principled stand on 'scientism's' behalf. Oh yes --- nought can brook progress' hand. We'll say this first man's given us full right of attorney – why, he's made a living will in death. HA! HA! Furthermore, Adam has also agreed to leave his wormy cadaver to medicine – all of it in accord with the Anatomy Act from the eighteen thirties." Momentarily, Doctor Pickford spies his assistant's reluctance to agree. "Sign the form!", he demands aggressively. "We are joint pioneers in flesh's signature." To the sound of which a biro scraped across this parchment like a snail moving on sandstone.

"Excellent", coos a younger man who's exhilarated by his performance. "Pass over my medical bag, will you? I refute 'ageism'… I come as the Lord's scourge. In terms of time's folly, my pouch contains an ichor or *elixir vitae*. It rolls back those years; it turns away the sun from its dials; it binds Nessus with Hercules' shirt."

Adam gazed on helplessly from one of them to the other. Like a lamb – he amassed nothing but slaughter's tokens.

TWENTY-FIVE

"Master, I heard the blow to our chamber's roof too. No, there's nothing to worry about in this dimension, I concurr. Any tremors which grow bypass us from the outside… especially given those turbulent gestures that reverberate continuously. Truly, our compact with heaven measures divinity's majesty thereafter. Isn't it a case of Zeus' living lightening?" Forthwith Adam's hand – which holds the intercom – appears to be misshapen. It heightens the dislocation of three toes, but now they are on one's mitten and beholden to a mollusc. Purple it happens to be – after the fashion of those tints on Greek sculpture, when, in their finery, they were buried beneath the Acropolis after Persian trespass. Aren't all civilisations based on *strata* of prior power that intrude on destiny – rather like mortal geology? One recalls Newton's jeremiad which came about as a consequence of scientific praise: "I saw further because I stood on giant's shoulders", he said. But Adam's face looked calloused, monstrous and even oafish – albeit with an antediluvian aspect. What can we tell concerning a criminal taint *a la* Lombroso or even Maslow's determinism? You are no doubt aware of the folk myth's ability to disclose a malefactor – simply by pertaining to a glance. It is the face, (you understand); especially in terms of both eyes' positioning. Our morphed Adam traded this trick again now; primarily by having a dewlap of skin covering over one eye. It fell down o'er a slip or a gibbet, and maybe it flapped in the wind as a portent? But whatever else did it signify? Did its left-sidedness preclude the evil eye; or otherwise lead it to wax sinister in accordance with tradition? A portent of the same grew up, though… for Adam has positioned around his neck a power amulet. It glistened heavily with a comparison due to yellow and red. It occurred way out of Madam Blavatsky's reach! Whereas Andalusia's green hand lay in his paw during her decease. Yet truthfully, didn't he intend to revive her to life (betimes); and even bequeath her his conscience *en passant*?

TWENTY-SIX

By a process of simulacrum our geriatric patient has almost passed out. Perhaps blessed sleep had come to him as a healing balm! Let's indulge our fissure or imagination for a moment… now that Doctor Pickford and Carruthers-Smythe are warming to their tasks. Who can essay such a Medusean fray as this? For no Perseus seems to be on hand in order to resolve the issue. Simultaneously with the above, then, Dr. Pickford moves with assurance along eugenic lines… even though any rhapsody spoken of re-interprets Gyorgy Ligeti's *Dance of Death*. More than ever so – because our Vincent Price has decided to inject our patient with his truth drug. It exists in a small syringe or pipette which thereby drains 'it' away into a fist; the latter gnarled in its rectitude or abundance. Carruthers-Smythe assists with the task – if only barely to the side – and by placing his hand firmly over the oldster's arm. It acts either as a clamp or as uncertainty's refuge (most probably). When behind this temple of conjoined flesh – or threeways to its necessary division – one detects a black screen. It comes down to head height like a private cinema… Nonetheless, a stray beaker, an ampoule or a tumbler lies behind such a project – all of which stands out nakedly against the sleek wooden surface of his bedside table (at once abridged to its rest). There was no need for our senilitic to move, however, since he's half asleep already… both due to a narcotic agent in the filter or phial, but also as regards the last hour's stress. Certainly, he hardly lets out a cry while the drug penetrates his stick-arm. Immediately in this operation's vicinity, however, Doctor Pickford's medical case came to be observed. It proves to be a peculiar kit with orange padding around its perimeter or surround, top and bottom, as was found in the base as well as the roof of a folding cabinet. Various pipettes, longitudinal spasms, drug allotments, syringes, enema devices and other levers of power clutter up this bag. A vague moan then becomes observable from our experiment's subject. Might he be Zenda's prisoner; or some more steely-like creature? But oh yes (!), this wonder drug is beginning to have its impact... undoubtedly so.

TWENTY-SEVEN

At the instrument's receiving end our thirty-first century Pickford signs off. Genetically speaking, he's relatively unchanged... although a rolled-neck pullover (of the darkest hue) indicates a stylish shift. This receiver or auto-link, a tiny mobile 'phone, remains in his hand. It embodies a rare air-trumpet – at least when turned around on a 78s logic and let loose. A grid – divided into segments or squares – then rises up in one's decisive latitude. It depicts valleys, greenness, temperate spaces and much else. Occasionally this virtual reality screen shudders – as if its presence was febrile, miscast or unreal. All in all, it replicates a mild off-cut from one of William Gibson's novels. Again, the doctor's features grow familiarly: with each crustacean of bone representing a splicing where two skulls combine, neck to neck. They are Carruthers-Smythe and Pickford --- together as one. While the retinas, for their part, twinkle coldly over pale skin, jet-black hair and a Leonine moustache. He continues to look at the device just spoken into...

TWENTY-EIGHT

Now comes our change... since Adam has begun to alter his eternal nature. 'It' spins – occasionally on the rebound – only to cross new fastnesses or to betray the intentions of R.S. Thomas' livery. The aged one's skin becomes less pale and it swivels to pink; thence fastening on so many lines' absence. Don't you detect its worthy notice? Especially in a scenario where the heads lolls back on the pillow; if only to reconnoitre bravery or find itself lost. Yes: the hair's innate greyness recedes and each strand thins out via a youthful day's approach. Similarly, the pillows behind his head look plumper or they seem to be more grey amid blue's dexterity. Certainly, these wrinkles slowly alter like a crab moving sideways after Cancer's sign which scuttles up the beach… and nearly always sideways-on. Observe this recurrent sentinel – for deep lines vanish with startling speed, while vitality flashes its stroboscope! Furthermore, a galvanic flush creeps over cheeks that were once ague's plague. Mightn't it all tie up – in terms of Edward de Bono's jumps – with Sir Arthur Conan Doyle's story *The Creeping Man*?

+

Whereas, in Pickford's estimation, a mime *artiste* intrudes into his imagination. The vision continually comes in at this point… because a new configuration ensues within the pineal eye. It shows a clown or a mask-like face when covered all-over with white grease-paint. Also, this figurine sports some belt and braces; together with a T-shirt of black stripes which rest across one's longitude. The face is capped by a red scallop and it's of a sort that encloses it within a bowl; i.e., at once leering to the skin or by way of a painted mask. Like bats circling in the wilderness or under your eaves, he screams in order to see… Yes, even a cry can mushroom at this moment, but it's still withering to know.

TWENTY-NINE

Our revelation continues, though, with Adam tilting forwards in his bed. Aren't you aware of a corpse's dalliance (?); whereupon a once prone cadaver rises up suddenly in order to release gasses within it. They were probably combustions or reactions inside one's corse… all of which is after a manner that recalls Barbusse's descriptions in *Hell* (most intrusively). Again, the cranium is free of its cushions now; in a situation where his red shirt appears more scarlet and the mop of grey hair less strained. Truly – like one of those speeded-up botanical photographs –

Pickford's serum was causing Adam to shed his years. They fall from him like a Joker's pack of cards! When repetitively, the mimer reappears and merely gestures with his thumbs up – all of it against a bright blue background. He holds up both his index fingers in gloved digits; at least when pursuant to LeCoq's theory and practice… Let one see it relieved (thus): in that the simplicity of performance apes at relief's index – particularly in a playlet where we are free to behold silence's art. Can it be a reverse threnody within the enactment of one's film?

+

During this endeavour small circular pulses or bubbles revolve around Adam's opening eyes. They detract from mayhem's affidavit; while, Stanley Spencer-like, our dotard continues to rise from his water-bed. --- Take up your bed and walk (!) … where have we heard such phrases before? Suddenly, a bright effulgence clears Adam's head; and it haloes him in a golden glow as he begins to speak. "Doctor", he starts by lisping via a croak, "I beg you to stop the serum prior to its biting too deeply. You don't understand the implementation of such a care. It will only resile from death's absence by opening the flood-gates (thereby). I entreat you to think before you liberate this course. It is not a game or a jeremiad you're playing; albeit after the signature tune of a television drama like *The Wild, Wild West* (for example). No. Try and reverse it, stop it or momentarily alter its transformation. Nothing but dysgenics can result from this plunge or dive. You see, I adopted this old or shrivelled form which was waiting to die many years ago. It renovated the illustration of a Colin Dexter novel called *The Riddle of the Third Mile* in all its livery and purposes. Whereby an eviscerated corpse is delivered to various victims when cut into pieces… all of it pursuant to blackmail or past infractions. Surely you remember its motif (?); i.e., a medical head and shoulders that were barely marked with surgical lore – or they resembled Gray's *Anatomy* when peeping out from straw. It came surrounded – in turn – by some rudimentary packing cases from "Bishop's Removals" in Wokingham, if not bloodied hammers betimes! Don't upend this signal, Pickford! Why don't you bear forth instead – when bleeding from life's whole – Cassandra's warning which concerns those furnished nets? Namely, these were the ones that caught Agamemnon within ichor's steaming bath. Heed whatever tumbrels disfigure you (thereby). I utilised old Adam's body deliberately; primarily so as to conceal what lay beneath. His real name happened to be Adam Bartholomew Jefferson, did you know? But let it ride – if I become younger and younger, as you desire, my true self shall stand revealed or wax naked *avaunt* this dawn. Assuredly, should I revert back my younger form will burst an amniotic surface and penetrate to such a level from below. Nor is that all. Since, in these circumstances, truth telling must go on to beget Armageddon after the fashion of a thousand flies. Those who wait outside can see me then. That's the signal; the unholy margin of fate. Once my true partiality's out – it provides a sign-post for the watchers. They shall observe and act. For when I morph into my true formula a starting pistol gets released. My metamorphosis bewitches any and all futures. Nor can it be dismissed – after Kafka's example – with the idea of transubstantiation into a beetle or suchlike grubs. *Mecynorrhina Polyphemus* can be dealt with! On the contrary, however, this idiolect may reform Babel's Tower after Breughel's observations. It has to be the end. *C'est Fini.* Prevent me from changing; it's a clapper-board or a notifying firework *for them.*"

+

With which clarion (then) Adam slumps back in his bed tired and exhausted. All of this was despite his growing youthfulness – whether page by page, hour by hour, minute by minute or hair-on-wrist by pulsating second!

THIRTY

Adam's voice seemed to be hoarse and distant now. Regardless of which – he still continued to warn and cajole. Mightn't this be the imprecations of one so damned? "I told you", he repeated, "you have to prevent such a transformation. Resile from it – I beseech you. It's still never too late. No instantiation can ever really interfere… leastways not with an eagle circling above. We are at modernity's final vista, doctors. Surely it resembles Boccioni's sculpture entitled *Unique Forms of Continuity in Space* from 1913? It trundles towards us with 'seventies flares portending much movement and wrapped o'er with speed – even immediacy. Act now in order to prevent disaster's unravelling…" During this outburst Pickford and Carruthers-Smythe remain strangely perplexed. One stood to the right of the other with a constellation of yellow or fluorescent lights above – when contrasted with a blue window out back. "I don't like it, Pickford", mouthed Carruthers in alarm. "Just listening to old Adam sounding off in this way; why, it gives me an attack of the screamers! It disables or causes alarm without any sanction. What does it mean?" The younger white coat of the two looked more sanguine. He merely shrugged his shoulders. "Don't be perturbed, my good fellow. His reaction keeps to normalcy's fellowship under sanctioned medication. After all, he's simply delirious. You don't want to join the company of Christopher Marlowe's *The Jew of Malta*, do you? Where – to quote from one of Washington Irving's stories – bogles and spirits don a night-cap only to flit about."

THIRTY-ONE

Again and again, Adam imprecates them in a sobbing whisper or spout, and it's one that finally ceases with a gurgle. Why do two texts come into one's mind; and these are Dalton Trumbo's *Johnny got his Gun* and L.P. Hartley's *Facial Justice*? Both deal resultantly with meat's manipulation… primarily amidst a burst of soul engineering. Finally though, Doctor Pickford is seen to be wide-eyed or in profile, and he's staring at Ovid's chest of drawers. Adam's ditty has trailed away now; it masquerades as an intruder in its dust. He hardly assaulted anyone with an empty boxing-glove, by the by. No. His last testament hissed the following: "Forget these fates. Yesss… I tried to warn you. No symposium can surrender to a bat's warriorship (thereby). For, in this very moment, I'm changing back through the glass of non-identity to what I once was. It cavils against my veriest doing or undoing. I liked your species, *homo sapiens*, not much – but enough to want to save you. A Latin tag… *fiat experimentum in corpore vili*. Now a land of falling towers awaits your evolved apehood. You see, this transformation bounds on apace and I revert to my true form. Correspondingly, no disguise will haunt my keen *anomie*. All alienations shall consequently end with this one. Have you ever consulted Emile Durkheim's monumental study on suicide? It were better if you had done so; lest you face unarmed what is to follow one's genesis. Too late… P..ickford; too late, doctor death. Those about to fulfil Eric von Daniken's prognosis; why, they salute you! All too l-l-late…"

+

But Pickford luxuriates ecstatically and like a candle in the wind. "You observe, Carruthers-Smythe, that I was right to press ahead. For this change of life proves to be upon us… it happens to be like a cosmic menstruation or the tide's alteration. I aspire to knock over your pig-headedness by way of daunt and dash. It works (I do declare); this serum labours and delivers, I tell you. Adam has recovered or rediscovered his long-lost youth. Eureka! A Nobel prize awaits me…"

THIRTY-TWO

Yet all must turn on occasions like this to ashes in the speaker's mouth…. since Adam had indeed been rematerialised. Why so? Because our young creature has become a *little green man*. His eye-sockets were shrunken within a space's expanse or delta, and both of them appear to be basins inside the skull. Do they have occasion to reinterpret a Frank Herbert monstrosity from *Dune*? No sir – even though these apertures are unseemly, rounded, gaping, tubular and unduly redolent of the word 'hole'. Each of them takes up a cranium's levelling; whereas – in contrast – the nostrils wax barely discernible on their apex. Nothing hints at a frieze's articulation (thereby); at least in a situation where a brow coruscates over some staring, limpid eyes. Great flabby ears – of a delicate emerald – stick out from the head… all of which occurs without any semblance or relief. Whereupon the alien's mouth stands open, louche, toothsome and even preternaturally alert. Still – the lower jaw hangs slightly in its protuberance from the rest of this offering. One must also mention the neck (betimes); in that it happens to be folded over like a turkey cock's. Against which Adam's formerly red-shirt holds out – rather translucently – and amid the stillness of a jet-black screen. What colour of green do we infer from this; irrespective of any Hibernian extract? Well, we will have to take on board a sap tint; at once mulcting to citrus and by way of chromium oxide. Also – olive, ochre (green), permanent, pthalo, turquoise (greenish), light, emerald, deep and Hooker's tints come up --- all of these need to be taken into account.

THIRTY-THREE

For an instant both Doctor Pickford and Carruthers-Smythe look dismayed – or even distraught. *Touché*. They hadn't reckoned on this drama turning into a *Twilight Zone* episode. Nor was Kingsley Amis' history of science fiction at all relevant here – despite the reference to a hundred Richard Matheson stories. (This isn't to mention Theodore Sturgeon's affidavit in such a committee of one hundred). Might a Hollywood film like *The Invasion of the Body Snatchers* atone for such a loss? Or could the latter be seen as an anti-communist satire – never mind its Khazar theodicy?

+

Pickford and Carruthers-Smythe continue to stagger backwards throughout. They are quite clearly dumbfounded by this turn of events. A beam of translucent light which barely cascades to yellow's pitch crosses over the room's advent now. Remember – darkness has fallen in a ward otherwise entrusted to one's task. By virtue of the fact that – in memory's origination – Adam had dallied on a general circuit, but he was then directed to a separate cube. This combination served as an examining room. Yet also, and in order to avoid prying eyes, Doctor Pickford has opted to use his serum on Adam's husk in a private dice. It proved to be an oblong which came shaped to the building's side; as well as being situated way up on a top floor. The mustard rectangles of this *bric-a-brac* crossed over, primarily so as to grant some squares and illumine those within. An interesting side-light of which meant that the medicos uniforms (hitherto white) turned black through the sun's reverse effect. Carruthers, the senior's assistant, is likewise backing away across this islet… while clutching at his neck and tie convulsively. Already his glasses – from the nineteen fifties and heavily reinforced – have slipped down nostril-wise. Perhaps also, if he started to grasp his head's back in abandonment (sic) then he could be nursing a thyroid wound? Meanwhile, "Adam's" bed remained dishevelled or unkempt, however, and a nearby chair found itself gripped by some green digits. They were decidedly sinuous in character. It was Pickford though – otherwise known as *doctor death* – who is the most spiritually troubled by these changes. He twisted and shook his crown; almost as if he'd been emboldened by some nightmare world! Maybe an unconscious cavern had opened up for him (?); whereby stoicism has fled full tilt into Labisse's cosmos. Or – more pertinently – must a lifetime's commitment to rationalism come full circle in a scenario where one's only response to the bizarre can be lycanthropy? Anyway, Pickford was heard to scream: "It is impossible – do you hear, Carruthers? It traduces every ladle of admitted science. Credulously, Sir Isaac Newton scripted various books on occult lore… each one of them reminiscent of *The Temple and the Lodge* by Baigent & Leigh. Yet he lived in an era which combined Roger and Francis Bacon… or even magic's template over experimental *doxa*. Have you ever consulted Professor Thorndike's *History of Magic and Experimental Science* in eight volumes from Columbia university press? It traversed Pliny's observations until at least the seventeenth century… For such illicit mixtures were implicit then. But NOOOOOO! (he looks again at the green'un). It's got to be an hallucination or utter madness!"

THIRTY-FOUR

Suddenly the hospice's top storey found itself illumined by a dazzling flash. It came from outside. Since – irrespective of a homily scene where low-rise buildings intersect in suburbia or are occasionally punctured by a passing Volkswagen – a weird craft jets into view now. It hovers teasingly above the building and is surrounded by others of its ilk. Such a ship betokens a classic flying saucer of yore – what with a cylindrical oscilloscope which was as flat as a pancake allows. While its discus arabesque recalls a Myron without hands and feet, or is pursuant to a million unidentified flying objects. Doesn't it incarnate a billion UFOs (?); and this was never mind government research in order to track them down. It seems to be constructed from platinum or a lost semblance of steel, and it reminds us of Gerry Anderson's television series *UFO*. Yessss... each vehicle casts off in a red frisbee's direction; together with blue 'windows' and a sensory projectile that looms beneath this skimming coin. For all the world it looks like an ant-eater's sprout – albeit one which has been constructed from metal. It appears to be searching out aught amiss... possibly given some signal or other. Whereupon it becomes obvious over whether these vessels are propelled by powerful launchers or boosters which were situated in their rears. Clearly they happen to be a thousandfold more advanced than contemporary or mortal science. All Carruthers-Smythe can do was to interrupt his colleague's mental breakdown. He fidgets nervously by a window. "D-Doctor Pickford, look, out yonder on this tube and amid a darkling sky, we're inundated by a Martian invasion. Isn't this our very own *war of the worlds*?"

THIRTY-FIVE

Within the alien space craft, however, all remained calm. Because, *ceteris paribus*, little green men go about their business or duty, and their task is imperialism. It proved to be undoubtedly so... Note: in this particular scene four emerald mugwumps gather around a telescreen in order to observe. Two of them have their backs to us. They are thirty-five milliseconds short of a universal excuse (in other words). Never mind: *quod* the dials around them whirl and click – when pursuant to so much grief. Interestingly, their shoulders were hunched over with almost Quasimodo's glee… whilst twin ears stick out in green beige (somewhat figuratively). Furthermore, their heads round themselves off to a shiny point; at least when viewed from behind. Whereas the aliens' dress consisted of a purple tunic or smock which was vaguely reminiscent of a Romanist priest. One of the creatures turns towards us now and he resembles our post-Adam. Might this have been a blasphemy against Levi-Strauss' *The Savage Mind*? Or alternatively – could the grinning skull, green carapace, cavernous eye-sockets and loose lips not signify one of Ensor's masks… albeit when abreast of an iron front? (This controlled sigil dates from 1888). Nonetheless, a species of dial or a whirling clock seems to counter-point our monstrous crew… Whereupon a planetary digit turns a nodule or spool, primarily so as to activate a scanner whose beam penetrates *all.* "Observe", says the anti-Adamic in his own language, "after a century or more our agent contacts us. He lets out a shout that fills the Heavens with wonder! Isn't it a clarion call *Against Nature*, if we are to make use of the mortals' novelist Huysmans? Too true: our advanced guard has abandoned his earthly guise in order to reveal aught. After Ibsen's *Enemy of the People* – truth frees destruction's fangs (you see). It releases the Four Horsemen! Truly, it must be our tocsin or signal… globally speaking."

THIRTY-SIX

"Listen to me", registers the lead ship's commander, "contact all our fleet. Communicate with every vessel. Instruct the entire flotilla or armada… and designate them thus: *procrastinate no longer*. Our terrestrial spy (hitherto disguised) has broken cover. Lead in all those armed discs that have been waiting for one hundred and fifty years. We know now – thanks to Adam's cunning – that it is safe to land and CONQUER EARTH!"

THIRTY-SEVEN

"Grieving helps not the wretched" – Seneca's chorus in *Hippolytus*

With this wave after wave of flying saucers descend upon the planet. They pour down from the blue clouds above and spray death from their nose-cones. Soon purple and brackish smoke begins to billow forth – all of it coming from flashes of flame which light up the ground. Greek fire illuminates everything (thereby); as human screams become admixed with a holocaust! (Wasn't this just a word that meant destruction by pitch, if used amongst elder Hellenes?) Before long the green-and-blue orb was ablaze. Yet amidst such End Times as these, transfigured by haze, the following scene took place. For – superimposed on each UFO or looming amid its impact and the sky – stood a SIXTY-FOOT DOLL. It embodied Andalusia's deportment.

HER LIPS WERE RED>HER SOCKETS VACANT>HER SKIN GREEN>HER HAIR GOLDEN>HER LIMBS LITHE>HER EAR-RINGS & CHOKE AMBER>HER BIKINI ORMOLU>HER LEGS LONG>HER VAGINA BARELY COVERED>HER LOIN CLOUT PEARLESCENT>HER CLOAK FLAMINGO>HER HEELS HIGH>HER NAILS TAPERING>HER VOICE LIKE A BELL!

Who might she be? Well, future anthropologists will call her a Goddess for little green men!

FINI

STINGING BEETLES
a dream

Cast of characters: These are Mezzanine Spratt, a travelling salesman and adventurer, together with Tanith Carpentier, a heroine, plus two mages named Biff and Boff. Various emanations of these thespians also zero in (spiritually speaking). The text will make this clear throughout. Likewise, Lord Talbot deserves a special mention. He was Anton LaVey's spiritual advisor on Roman Polanski's *Rosemary's Baby* – although a revisionist ouija board had disembarked Ira Levin early on.

(Author's remarks: this is a story about diabolical possession).

I
Mezzanine Spratt, the main puppet in this particular roadshow, has been dreaming.

II
Tanith Carpentier began by thinking aloud: "The rain drops have stopped beating in their plentifulness – albeit primarily on an empty screen. A wind-screen, I mean... Nonetheless, Mezzanine Spratt has definitely crumpled over with tiredness. His red convertible had almost left the road a while back. Was it either driver error or fatigue? Possibly both... but, in his imagination, something more distrait proved to be happening.
+
For he is sitting at a masquerading table which was basically lit up by multiple candelabra. These festooned the dining-room, and this appears to be despite the wind and water that lashed without. A rare dispersal of goods lay down on this special linen – some of these items in silver salvers or rare pewter jugs. Didn't the candle-light glisten off them rather spectacularly? A bowl of fruit became discernible now; while various tureens of meat or fish occasionally came forth. In the background there seemed to be a pump-room or some sort of wax-work museum. At least a fix-

tide of industrial machinery – with large brick kilns in evidence – tidied up one's gloom. At one end sat Tanith with a plunging bust, pearls and a pair of banqueting gloves. A cock-tail glass – at once stick-rolled – lolled between her gloved fingers. At the other end or projection nestled Mezzanine… irrespective of the fact that he looked strangely altered. He had become monstrously disfigured or otherwise discouraged (you see). His face comes across as mobile, waxen, labile and even viscid. Can you detect this transformation? Moreover, his visage kept bobbing up behind a vista of flaring candles. It always shimmered to a stare or hid aslant whitefish water. Yet Mezzanine Spratt's Cycladic mask betokened the unmistakable (thereby). It certainly ripped off any semblance to nonesuch – even though he could have been suffering from hyperpituitarism or some similar malady (most assuredly). Yes? Since the man's physiognomy comes contained in a bubble made of plexiglass – if only to then characterise the Halloween mask of his face. For surely it crepitated or ran in new pits of distortion (?); and it smiled like a crab-apple. Might it have the bends or be smeared by a blow-torch? Anyway, its acromegalic displacement fitted a new moral ugliness; the like of which was held aloft by an exo-skeleton (though it be). This suit's binary colours were red and blue… they stood for hot and cold, you know?"

III

Mezzanine Spratt, his head lolling like a broomstick, ruminated the following: "I must have passed out for a brief travail betimes. After all, one bit of road resembles another one under these conditions. All remains indeterminate via a blank screen such as this. But still, don't I recall a restaurant's rendezvous with no butler or flunky available to gesture to? The candles flickered or pirouetted abreast of me in their holders as before. Also, my face bequeathed its hideous gesture just like a past entreaty. Didn't it encode sundry luncheon meat – when vacuum-packed – and somewhat rare in its prominence? I reached across only to unscrew the lid on a bottle of claret. Hmmm…, was that really the stew? To be certain of our ground, though: I swivelled the contents in an ice-bucket which unfolded unto this last. *Touché*, these flaring candles lay between my darling, Tanith, and myself. Most definitely, she looked ravishing tonight in her little black number with the plunging neck-line. The alcohol flowed into her glass thus disfiguring the Irish crystal – if only to renounce a pout. Do you know what I'm saying? Because she didn't move from her chair during this entire performance. Let's look at her more closely: in that her blonde hair cascaded down in reefs, her eyebrows were arched and the girl's teeth are pearly in their whiteness. Surely it's a *MacClean's* sunrise all round, then? The eyes, however, wax azure, jet blue, orb-like and come to reinterpret marbles. Could they be false in their entreaty or otherwise legging it to paradise? Since Tanith – in this incarnation – was a waxen effigy or a manikin. Hadn't I discovered her in a waxworks factory like Madame Tassaud's? Ye-s-s-s-sss. I hissed aloud now… when altogether locked into a possessive glare. I leant over my beloved in a delicate fashion – with the candle-sticks still spitting and sending out stroboscopic 'heat'. I adjusted the liquor and my brillo-pad head came to be burnished in the flame… as it passed over from one reality into another."

IV

The mages have gathered in order to inspect their prey from above. "My shadow-brothers, all goes as we planned or surmised it. For Mezzanine lies slumped over in the pit or amphitheatre of his car. Let us look to the side… wherein rivulets of water criss-cross the screen beyond our ken. Each mote or scratch of H(2)O then blackens one's transept before it passes aft. This was despite one special instance… namely, when the wipers stutter at the outermost circumference of their circle prior to passing back. But we can descend deeper or down alongside these heart-felt dreams – isn't it so, my brothers?

+

Whereupon a hominid who was accustomed to a lit parade sat still for a moment. His measure may be found out by those candles; at least when each one is metered sequentially from the next. They lay along a table's middle or rested thence in accordance with its brevity. Every one of them flickered within a kaleidoscopic burst… out of whose flames his disfigured head can be seen to bob and weave in a bubble. An incident of many years before now came up – albeit matured by his mind's eye. In it he was seen to walk along with a beautiful babe who proved to be blonde of hue, and they were exiting from one night-spot or other. All too readily, though, various persons in their vicinity had begun to scatter or flee. What went on throughout this; or have they begun to study his face, perchance? Because – at a later date and under the fluffy bow-tie – it has started to melt. Is it deliquescing or discombobulating bit by bit? Whereat, and like the unmasked visage of Gaston Leroux's *Phantom of the Opera*, one rip or tear reveals an unripe plum that vegetates behind a balaclava's indifference. Does an objective observer know – however unsteadily – whether such an image relates to Lord Raglan's Crimean campaign? Too true, old man… since one's pericarp came blinded to a geyser like this or it's liable to meld like clay – especially while pursuant to a forgotten regime. Did it possibly relate to hygiene at all? By virtue of which and beneath the girl's outraged or stilleto'd feet, when glued to the pavement, Spratt's flesh had cascaded down after some viscid rheum and when merely given over to kissing one's ground. Slowly she swooned in an itemised cocoon now that her date has melted on the spot… thereby representing a Toblerone or a triangular chocolate if subjected to a naked flame.

+

Throughout all of this the moon reflected its abundant light; at once calm, gibbous, mesmeric, held-in, enraptured and cool."

V

Mezzanine Spratt had folded himself over in order to sleep in his vehicle. "I am speeding on now beyond the temple of one's dreams. Yes indeed, I lie semi-comatose in my car… even though these head-light beams of mine can barely cut through this darkness. All of which proves to be irrespective of any water that cascades and pings off metal! No sir… but the grip of dream-time or its somnolence is upon me. Can't you grapple with its craggy outer limits, my friends? First up, my melting sickness seems to have led to hospitalisation – yet not in any expected capacity… For aren't I outside the intern faculty or its wardship, and looking in? Assuredly so, I leap in a fleet of foot manner towards a casualty department which has been lit up from the outside-in. Certainly, no-one really wants to configure what I might have become or evolved into. To tell you the truth it all means nothing to me whatsoever, but I do remember the expectations of a vault or a scenario where, unlike the two public school-boys in *Arthur Seaton's Aunt*, I leapt towards my fate!

+

Touché! Didn't my hooves ricochet from a parked laundry vehicle by way of this darkness – while arching up towards nothing other than a black space? I catapulted myself upwards through some jagged shards which were themselves illumined by false balsam or an echoing yellow. Must one substantiate the matter further? Anyway, my feet ground upon the hospital's carpet and crunched it underfoot – particularly now it was covered over with the window's sward. Then again, I should possibly have wondered why this aperture is wide open before I'd arrived. Never mind… since I crouched down pursuant to any utterance and prior to leaving off. Ahead of me lay Biff with an enormous laser-ray in his armoured fist. Truthfully, he wore a dark-green cape around his frame; itself steel-clad and velvet-made like a mediaeval knight adorned with the latest gadgets. But these gewgaws aside and bestrewn around the place… something struck me with main force between the eyes! Inevitably, wasn't there a connexion between this skull-head and a past one which had grown all magisterial? *Quod* haven't I gone abroad rather masterfully and in blue vestments, but without Sir Henry Irving's self-confidence? You know that he was the greatest Victorian actor, I presume…? Leastwise, Bram Stoker turned out to be an able amanuensis in his two-volume *Reminiscences of Henry Irving*.

+

Nonetheless, a striking similarity grew up between Biff and me – at least in terms of my palsied existence under a glass-dome that had been wrapped around the head. Oh so mercifully now… don't you summon up Brian Aldiss' novel *Barefoot in the Head* instead? To be certain of our time, O want of blood: Biff wore a helmet containing antlers like a pterodactyl's ferment – especially when occasioned by matching bones. Perhaps it came to vent what Arthur Koestler called *The Act of Creation* (?); or it wanted some dysgenic plastic thereby. It definitely appears that he wore about him some animal skin or pelt, and even luxuriated in an absent purchase from this vista. Necessarily so – since lying redundantly upon the floor or before his weapon lay Boff. Could it have been a residual emanation, though? Anyway, it happened to be a dwarf or one of the little people! Yet – within such a semblance of pain – weren't Biff and Boff supposed to be allies? No matter: this daemon's gun waxes jammed; and wasn't it only a vaudeville blunderbuss to begin with?"

Biff, who momentarily speaks through a mouthful of fish, masks up slowly. "My fluted rifle has misfired! How can this be? What outermost purpose or drama – in one's ethics of misplacement – gels with any metaphysics which go on here? Didn't the Jew or the Son of Man whom the Romans crucified at the Pharisees' behest want to declare that everything has a purport, even as it relates to two birds falling to the ground? You see, it must be the metaphysical objectivism of all metaphysical objectivisms… especially after the fashion or interregnum of Julius Evola. May one consult without compulsion his revolutionary codex which makes war on modernity in the name of tradition? *Radex*, you infer… he wishes to return to the root or to one's blood-in-the-bone abreast of its spectre."

Boff has been reduced to a midget by dint of mixed breeding. For all miscegenation helps to illustrate a bounty of decay. His voice measures the following… "He must have fled from us, O my brothers… primarily after the failure of his sten gun to fire. Didn't you notice it? Yet he speeds from us – merely expectant to his need – and in order to avoid fatality's arrest. Let's recognise the way he chooses to run when pursuant to nought save self-interest and hemmed in by aluminium. He moved laterally with his cape veering behind him or seen as an architectural slide. Might it embody a Pop Art vestibule by Rauchenberg or a still frame from von Stroheim?"

VI

Mezzanine Spratt ran slantwise in the rain and always in accord with one vehicle or t'other. He spoke solemnly to himself in mesmerism's grip. "I leap abroad when attendant on deliverance, but not without pain. Or maybe it has to do with the end result or its prognosis (?); I forget which. Suddenly the dwarf's outstretched boot seeks to trip me or to send me sprawling on the linoleum… otherwise constructed from *lapis lazuli*. Can't it be construed as slippery in the extreme?"

Boff holds his gaiter up high in contemplation of the void. He declares. "Huuuuussssshhhh, miscreant… listen to me well! Your involvement in this case is unwanted, unheralded, sprightly and without either terms or offering – leastwise given such a spirit of sacrifice. Yonder intervention cannot be wished for, do you see? Any fight that you seek to delve into or relish doesn't want your presence…"

Mezzanine Spratt replies in high dudgeon. "Wrong, my friend, the gander is up or all troubadour tunes have broken out of their fastness. Don't I fling myself forward and somersault in mid-air before landing laterally? I then run off in the direction of some competent store-rooms; if only to throw my body outwards like a commando. Certainly, a trapezoid of light fizzes across this emerald corridor and it showers down a mezzanine's effulgence. Whereas each parallel bar of 'sound' infracts upon a grey door – the cast of it embodies a cell. All of an instant a truckle-bed hurtles across a corridor from a neighbouring one. It speeds this way and that *avaunt* I bring it to a close with my foot. The blanket on the pallet remains a pale ochre – while the pillow's tint veers towards white by way of blue. Standard issue, I suppose… Anyway, the orderly looks suspiciously like Graham Sutherland, the Hollywood actor of yesteryear. 'What's vertical to this or pregnant in its depth-charge issue?', I demanded aggressively… 'Nought', he answered pensively with a token of sullenness. 'Yes', he continues without paying much attention. 'They're mere offices, residues of business or habitations to storage. Does one comprehend it?' In pursuance of which – I flaunt my vigilante status by hurling myself onwards without fear. Whereupon lines of force radiate around me after the details of a subdued battle or joust. Possibly though, it strives to inscribe death's rainbow colour by colour?"

VII

Biff, who looks into a green mirror that is limned with dark mould, speaks as follows. "He still stares out into the future – somewhat morosely. Might he be caught up in the cell or construct of his car? Wherein this automobile stands under a casement to those surrounding sheets of rain. Or could these be described, *en passant*, as volcanic heave-toes of ash which cascade from above? In any event, our travelling salesman decides to reverse his vehicle into a lay-by in order to grab a sun-dial's shut eye. A bank of deeply verdant trees surround his red convertible all a'drip. The dim sun has also descended on its sky-line…"

VIII

Mezzanine – when alive to an odyssey of humour – said the following. "Well, the store-front opened its offerings to me with a blank doorway marked 'do not enter' hiding some reddish

light. May it be chloroform or ether in an objectless space? Various bottles lie in squared cubicles – when packed away from lino to ceiling and in subdued tones. Not a hint was heard from these surroundings… Now Biff looked down with a scarlet bulb transfixing one's glow – almost as if he were part of a wall of sarcophagi whose faces were turned up. He wore antlers upon a handicap's brow throughout this turn…
Biff: "Mezzanine doesn't hear the prod of one's silence behind one. Nor need he grapple with anything too complicated; especially when fear laces envy with respect. Possibly a large bottle of formaldehyde which was mixed with pure ethanol crashes near him. Moreover, the conundrum of its explosion happens to be louder when it is confronted by stillness. Poisonous fumes are released thereafter. They vaporise and all of them collocate or build upon the budding air. Each swirl of driftwood lists towards yellow and it finds fault resultantly, or it troubles a witness over science's ready passion. In these Stygian vaults a thousand bottles can fall only to repeat a growing impediment to phantasy. Does one detect it? Since, in von Stroheim's original nine-hour epic *Greed*, the murdered Marina haunts Trina's dreams. (It all came from Frank Norris' naturalist or socio-biological novel *McTeague*). Whereupon Maria grapples with a fence; at once lemur-like and clutching at straws so as to gain her revenge. Might she become a Joker in her own pack of Aces?"

Tanith Carpentier: "My looking down on this scene has the solemnity of a dream or a female orgasm. Doesn't the latter have to do with a blueness, a serenity or an utter calm with one's partner… even a blanking out in the brain. Regardless of this – a whole constellation of vials and casks plummet downwards (thereafter). An enormous roar results when this heavy glass – minus its asphyxiation – finally hits pay-dirt. Biff grins on in the darkness. He has become mean-spirited, quite probably rapt and certainly blinded in one eye with inattention. Over his head he wears some fossilised bone – much after the fashion of Erich von

Stroheim in *La Grande Illusion* by Jean Renoir. Nonetheless, a hand can be seen flailing beneath this medicine… all of it having been released from its captivity in myriad ways. Even though Biff garners on amidships… He happens to be 'eyeless in Gaza only to see --- when blue-eyed --- what an exo-skeleton could muster.' Might it be the formulation of a Tryannosaurus Rex between-times – i.e., a T without the rest, eh?"

Mezzanine Spratt's *mea culpa* follows on shortly. "I am surrounded by gold bars – due to the fact that an entire packing case of lozenges has fallen on me. Or were they pushed from above? A detective's question – whether for Sherlock Holmes or Sexton Blake – if ever there was one… Despite this, though, I am determined to rise from this pit of haemoglobin which slides around after the fraction of a microscope's essay. Isn't the machine on full power in terms of its light source? Never mind: since ordinary minds are neutered by any determined ascent. Here I go again – for a lifted pillion must slake its thirst on this tarmac. Anyway, my carrion will never rustle up such undercooked meat. It has to rise – no good can come of pretending otherwise. Still and all, one's silhouette indicates an indifference to pressure of this sort. It promulgates itself and makes free-play of transcendence thereby. May one declare it over? Truly, my fist penetrates the balsa *et viola* (!) with one punch I'm free. Yet – to paraphrase Proudhon – liberty can never be constrained by a license on circumstances. No. For my form rears up when covered in liquid ether – the like of which runs off in rivulets. Are they unstinting in their praise? I clench my teeth, growl and gather about me a piece of wood in order to possibly use it as a weapon. Who knows? Yet underneath my beetling brows each eye had become a slit. Round about me a noxious reek of gas seeks to rise up and away; at once filling the space feverishly with its insecticide."

Biff stands fully adorned in a daemonic rig. "You have stood up, proud one, only to admit your defeat's luxuriance. Nothing awaits your spirit now but a Tarot card… the one marked death and that often indicates transformation or renewal. Discard all other discourses or mend the magic of forgotten days! Too true, your vanquished sigil comes covered in rheum or green-spirited; and is measured by blood's barometric pressure. Forget it not – because my pagan head bellows a kindred indifference towards our plight. Are you a stranger to a tabernacle of lost pain? Any road up, the very pterodactyl feel of my head-gear seeks the sun like Icarus in reverse. He flew too near one's glistening solar panel in Greek myth (you know). Its orb proved to be too strong, singed his wings and sent him plummeting to the turf beneath. Lo, but look, helmet and all, I have become Lord Talbot! He incarnates a very devil, demon or lower thaumaturge. May his green-spiked dome come forwards in an undefeated manner! What did Madame Blavatsky say about Lucifer's gift of fire to mankind in her *Secret Doctrine*? Might it wax promethean after Heraclitus' blessing?"

IX

Tanith Carpentier continued to comment on events via a distant haze. "Yes, he remains conscious in his diligence throughout. Too far it seems… Given the implementation of the following agreement: in that his head slipped down beneath the seat. Orange it was and with shiny appurtenances. Above all, the top-'n'-tailed trilby sunk down or delved towards a skull's irretrievable nature. What can he be thinking about? Why, merely that nought ever really happens to him; *viz.*, no excitement, chastisement or adventure occurs within. Do you see? Since no wife or woman waited up for him in the one-room apartment he called home. No sir… it wasn't a defeated architecture, but he did remain aware of the rain's pitter-patter. Its onomatopoeia enclosed sound's displacement or clatter, and it led onto some bullets' distribution!

+

Likewise, did he remember a scene of lost triumph? A scenario within which a waxen doll shone on as a blonde and under reflective lights – the latter occasioned by candles lit up to the nines. Further, her cupped ball-room gloves were enclosed so as to feast on a festival of fools… at least by dint of some lost wine. Whilst Mezzanine's cranium had become deathly or a death's-head (so to say). Now then, his living skull was spent and shrouded over to a brillo pad, or it existed under plexiglass. Its look became the leprosy of a new utterance – one that's destined to festoon the desks of an imagined Tarot. Whereas he wore around his frame a power-pack dedicated to solitude; itself liable to reinvigorate some spinal tap. The armour seemed heavy or unballetic in its choreography. It even insisted upon the notification of a new crusade. Yes… the masonism of this effort had to construe a purpose – primarily by means of an implosion *face-to-face*. But what did this amount to? For those candles which lit up a diner's scene… why, they have collapsed and cause naked flame to course along its linen. Within a matter of minutes the entire playlet is ablaze – as liquid pitch bursts out across this wax-work's façade. A neo-classic facia it always happened to be, but now it's incandescent with Greek Fire's descant. Why do you choose to doubt it? Yet from the outside how can a blonde figurine possibly go any further, even if she remains fastened to her seat as my *alter ego*? Certainly, she must melt into fluidity after a brave-time's bell, or when pursuant to crystal cracking. Won't it recall one of Boccioni's sculptures; if only fitfully unfurled before a wind-tunnel's silence? Even farther out can't Mezzanine snap his bonds and – like a robotic creature in the Capek brothers' play *RUR* – will he then hurl himself into this inferno? All to rescue his love… also, before one's explosive holocaust his face runs like liquid treacle within its mask or expectation (almost). 'Tanith, my love', he shrilled, 'don't despair… I'm coming for you!'

+

We then cut to the scene of an enormous explosion."

X

Mezzanine Spratt: "I wander towards this devil-doll which is adjacent to my studio vista. Moreover, its claws are transparent –

especially when seen through the thick etheric slaughter of one's mists. Against such thinking an oversight of orange gauze floats up from below; it's adrift of those shattered boards which came from the shelving roundabout. Before me stood Lord Talbot; at once grasping a stave before a savage iota of Halloween. Doesn't it declare itself to be a candle that flares within a pumpkin (?); the mouth, nose and eyes of which have been cut out with a knife. All of it has been recorded by some reflective dye, you know? Similarly, the demon afore me hissed out of a reptilian bastinado (possibly). It reared up like a green'un or when percussive to an old dinosaur's witness. On I surged as I sought to pummel it with my fists – but against its saurian armour no impact could I make. I blundered on in the half-darkness often keening at this rage or turret, and yet susceptible to change. Look at it now: my limbs felt heavy and over-burdened as I attacked. Could it embody the final conflict between Marcus and McTeague in von Stroheim's *Greed*? (A hemicycle that was filmed in California's death valley at the apogee of this particular sun). Unhesitatingly though, the pot-bellied significance of Biff came through regardless... Might it reallocate indistinctiveness' obesity or the sin of gluttony (?); thence having occasion to spin over into the half-light. It also indicated an inner connexion between Talbot and Biff. Weren't they the same daemonic entity (?); albeit masquerading behind a carnival's obsession with one harlequin's hanging. No matter: because the oval of such a belly helped to trap a variant on uncleanness, even if only circulating to grey now. Everything found itself held up within this dilemma. But soon I was down or flattened to Camus' *Fall* – primarily by one of those demonic blows. Talbot stood over me with 'its' nostrils twitching and snorting."

XI

Biff and Boff were speaking in unison as siamese twins. "Let us examine a plenitude of freaks, my brothers. For wasn't Caligula just an undivine child who's otherwise wasteful to its source (?); or liable to make his favourite horse into a Consul? Couldn't this be done by virtue of an alternative mission statement (?), even a grafted on treaty. Surely it would illustrate a reversal of Raoul Vaneigem's *The Book of Pleasures*, a decadent volume which advocates paedophilia?

+

To be evident about it: Mezzanine Spratt's head has slumped down into a trilby-laden seat. Indefinitely though, the pain or effulgence of this water almost cascaded through the glass... metaphorically speaking. Might it be an example of one pane favouring another before the gesture of these Norns (?) ... all of it occurring ahead of a northern wind. Remember that in another incarnation Spratt proved himself to be a tragic figure; i.e., one who merely sacrificed himself for the love of a waxen doll. All of this took place in a manner reminiscent of German expressionist cinema or von Stroheim's luridness. Out Hollywood way it was... wherein the gypsy-like Zerkow dreams (in *Greed*) of retrieving the ormolu dinner-service from a burial ground. His face during these shots found itself convulsed with a gross livery or beholden to an unholy love!

+

Mezzanine slowly revives. For a while he nearly rests his heavy chin on the steering-wheel. What to do next, however? Clearly, he can't snuggle up like this when pursued by dampness' residue. Since he primarily needs to quit this place or find solace in a boarding house nearby. A neighbouring hamlet could be a possibility... anyway, he slews the car around and heads off into these swirling undercurrents. May he now turn the vehicle's key, engage its starter, and feed petrol into its engine only to see it lurch onto a glistening road? Let's take this bishopric or diagonal movement in chess as far as it can progress."

XII

Tanith Carpentier gestures from afar like Gloria Swanson in *Sunset Boulevard* by Billy Wilder. Isn't she the Vamp's vamp, thereby? "Truthfully, I knew his absence would impart some renewal to this circle. Don't misunderstand me! Because do you see a *vampirella* in front of you – oppressed one of another existence? I constantly stride towards a basalt column which is just tempted over to sequin and idly lists forwards. Truly, a swirl shows up everything else. It occurs amid mist and many of my colleagues gather in a darkness well off to the west. Or shall it be a species of leftism, spiritually speaking? Needless to say, this *zeitgeist* has turned over on itself amidships. Didn't Julius Evola, the author of *Revolt Against the Modern World*, speak of a 'war of position' like a vesuvian chess match? Yess-s-s, since his gargoyle lolls over your cranium's side in a dragon's get-up or rig, and it merely waits to still such distempers. Its refusal looked like a dinosaur (perchance), or even a brontosaurus and a pterodactyl. It waxed turquoise in its delusion and waited to foment ichor from a creature's mouth.

+

Doesn't Lord Talbot leer over him now… with Richard Wagner's *Ring* cycle blaring away in the background? A dexterity that intimates nothing other than a claret sky – leastwise it carpets the space between them *avec* vermilion. No matter how brilliantly… since in a matter of moments Biff had become enormous. He dwarfed this tableau and wore a reptile's helmet throughout, and Talbot's covered over by intertwined bullet-belts. A cape masqueraded over one shoulder and it concerns a rampant dragon… the heraldic device or *imprimatur* of Talbot's house. Moreover, his grin came blackly etched from one of indifference's wounds or amid bleeding teeth. Slowly & surely Mezzanine's body was dragged outside through a door downstairs and across a yard. An alley cat, dressed in black-and-white fur, looked on inquisitively as Biff passed with Spratt. He shifted him roughly across these stones' keeping."

Biff: "Too true – I move apace of death with an elaborate weapon slung over one shoulder. An ambulance or a similar vehicle awaits me across the forecourt. But what is this? I look out through the blinded compassion of one eye; and it comes stilled via fish-bone or an amphibian's vertebrae. Can one comprehend it? Especially now that a hospital guard who is armed with a truncheon confronts me and asks about my business. Yet who can really analyse Talbot's inner motivations properly? Assertively, I am prepared to depart. Surely this orderly was one of Mezzanine's emanations (?); even though our impress waxes forgetful due to his wearing of a female mask. It comes to be characterised by gold (herein), or is painted red and green. One eyelet has tears beneath it. Maybe this androgynous touch bears upon it Tanith's impress? I curse 'it' in consequence..."

XIII

Mezzanine Spratt looks on from a dream's phantasm. "Here I am (*per se*) and my convertible has stopped abreast of a forest's advent. Still the rain-drops fall from the heavens – plus a breaking up of so many of these footsteps amongst trees which are lit up by lightning. A sky-space pokes out of such woods thereafter. Now it becomes clear to me – particularly through the whistling blade of my wipers – that a fork in the road has emerged. A Zeus-flash cuts across such living melancholy, if only to reveal two wooden signs set up starkly in the mire. Both are heavily constructed from horse-chestnut... but where, my good friends, do the conkers come in? One signification reads Maeohild; a ruse which doubtless refers to a heroine in Anglo-Saxon literature who almost pines to death from love. The *other*...? Why, it denotes Bhagwan or the crone's triple image who wears Kali's face. It indicates a feminine cult of death or eventual rebirth. Given all potential inferences like these – what road should one take? Simply because, in this life, you can only travel in one direction when confronted by such divergences..."

Bearing in mind all of the above, then, Mezzanine swings the vehicle around and heads down towards Bhagwan underneath these trees. All of them are dripping in their disclosure or half-light.

XIV

In such a metamorphosis Lord Talbot looks up at this hybrid guardian. Couldn't he/she be a misunderstood amazon? Yet finally, the transformation became complete and Tanith Carpentier stood aslant him. His stockinged legs were above his line of vision. They provided a momentary significance – especially given proceedings like these. Isn't this either the thirteenth or the fourteenth act under our proscenium arch? Moreover, weren't her legs tightly meshed or otherwise fish-netted with a pink residue? It betokened flesh (you see); and they faded into a turquoise awakening.

Lord Talbot/Biff: "You are here to gloat, then?"

Tanith Carpentier: "Gloating remains a victim's sacrifice without any glory."

Biff/Lord Talbot: "I wonder if you have the stomach to enable such a discharge."

Tanith Carpentier: "Quiet, old one... for the rain ricochets around your skull in spasms. If you remain silent for a moment between times – you'll hear it."

Lord Talbot/Biff: "Wretch, no wonder man has never trusted woman since Eden's garden. Indeed: nothing prelapsarian can rest easy until an adder makes its way up your leg."

Tanith Carpentier: "Flattery cuts no ice with those who are accustomed to a skinhead's autobiography. Do you remember the Golgotha which breaks up Holbein's *The Ambassadors* – no matter how elongated it might turn out to be? It comes replete with green velvet."

Biff/Lord Talbot: "All I can recall to memory were Savonarola's strictures on Renaissance painting (strictly speaking). Could he have been wise all along? For surely they came to be impregnated with a pagan lustre?"

Tanith Carpentier: "Your nonchalance intrigues me throughout. What force really lies behind ebon lines that are drawn on white vellum or in terms of runic inscriptions? Can a skilled mind read them with ease?"

Lord Talbot/Biff: "That is simple to essay – they belong to Bhagwan's curtain."

XV

Mezzanine Spratt: "The car stepped on the gas of a new provider, but never in terms of a misguided show. Still – between times – he steered through an abundant trap which existed down beneath these shimmering boughs. His hands continued to grasp an ungainly steering-wheel as it turned this way and that… while his thoughts fell pell-mell or all a'jumble! Whichever fork on life's road should one decide on, if we bear in mind its course into a vampire's heart? All of a sudden a dream-scape comes into his mind – it concerned Mezzanine Spratt plus a.n.other who was as yet undisclosed. Is it his imagination (?); or were they meeting in an office of bureaucratic fact? Can it have aught to do with patents or Crown copyright? Regardless of this – his *alter ego* lounged before him and he played poker using a brillo-pad face. Isn't it really habituated to megalomania – albeit over a rubbery jowl and an armoured suit of red 'n' blue? 'Good Lord!', declared our bubble-head. 'Where? Wheresoever can he be hiding, at least when pursuant to a new form of punctuation', I uttered in response. 'Oh, oooooooohhhhhhhhhh, I see, it's just a phrase… a term of endearment. Good, good… let's get ahead now.'"

I led my red convertible down a narrow track during a time when this memory receded from my face. Might it re-interpret Dog Lane from my childhood in Peppard… plus a country wench at its end? All lay sodden or roundabout this due. Furthermore, massive aspens and oaks towered around – or faced off against one another on every side. May it reassemble an Algernon Blackwood story known as *The Man Who Loved Trees*? The water sheeted down full pelt on occasion… and yet a coruscation of lightening illumined one's way. For – like Odin in a slouch hat – I wandered among my kindred. A wisp of smoke from a chimney – at once hidden behind these waving trees – struck out west. I drove in its direction.

XVI

Lord Talbot was wearing Biff's face over an amputated trunk. Had any surgery actually been involved? "*Avaunt thee*! The old fool – more masculine now – confronted me about this hospital's burden. We know the answer though! But we're not going to tell it yet… because our tale hasn't reached its desperate climax. Still, I have dragged my culprit across a white fastness only to leave his form stretched out. Hadn't the orderly been told that he needed assistance, if only to die? He bent down so as to confront confusion; leastways before I slapped his neck and caused him to fall. Whereupon I dragged Mezzanine backwards into an ambulance afore taking off at great speed. The vehicle sped on leaving dwarfish Boff, the attendant and another of Spratt's aspects in my wake. They recomposed themselves after having been covered with exhaust or carbon monoxide fumes. But Mezz(.) has regained his wind or valour now – primarily by kicking open the back door and plummeting out into space. Along his carrion flew above this noxious guff or floating in the draught. Turning aboutways, his simulacrum caught sight of a spectator: 'Master Spratt', he breathed.

XVII

Mezzanine Spratt kept driving onwards… while his gloved hands were fastened onto the wheel. What makes a man take one course of action rather than another? Sincerely, it had to do with the way the Norns arrange things for you. Some call it fate or karma.

Whereas Mezzanine continued to speed on; and this was basically oblivious to all crime or hazard. In these circumstances, he manoeuvred the roadster under a thunder-cloud. A burst of lightening lit up your foreground; a factor which was attendant upon a neglected point of view. Never mind… he'd heard of hurricane Katrina plaguing New Orleans so; and yet Mezzanine also knew that all 'progressive' notions fall sheer before nature's majesty. Since no-one can choose their race, ethnicity, eugenic capacity, disabled absence, non-semitism or Gentile status, class strand, sexuality, intellect, beauty or lack of such. You see, environmentalism or social causation proves to be catalepsy's lozenge. For everything subsists within a biological filter. Man is born and not made, in other words. A scenario whereupon cultural studies only replaces natural lore with a furnished definition. *Ceteris paribus*, marxism stands refuted by a single example of Zeus' thunder claps or bolts. Wasn't this all-father a master of our living lightning, thereby?

By estrangement's token, Mezzanine became aware of some lights on amid the trees. Surely a hamlet reared up amongst a sward otherwise washed clean by oblivion?

XVIII

She had seen him break free in order to seek succour from an oubliette. Alternatively, he sensed a one-eyed Cyclops emerging from the dark!

++

Biff, who was shading into Lord Talbot, zig-zagged towards some more trouble. "Here we go… for Mezzanine's figure lies recumbent in this gloom. Has it really left an ambulance's portal (?); or can he have sped through mortal doors by way of oblivion. He lay crumpled up in a heap. While another of his emanations – who happened to be dressed in an anorak – approached south-by-south-west. *Touché*! The fool, however, must be grasped in my collective lock and slammed into our vehicle's side… or never effectively let free. He drifted off towards the ground in a somnolent manner. We (or I) grasped his master and hauled him back into the medical van's recesses. Might it recall 'Doc' Holladay's legendary carriage out in the wild, wild west of yesteryear? Moreover, didn't the anarchist sloganeer Michael Bakunin once declare that he wanted to be *we not I…*? (A point which occurs in E.H. Carr's hostile biography). Further to such a template, though, a paramedic's omnibus roared off and it left a cloud of choking dust behind it."

++

Tanith Carpentier: "I facilitated your coming embrace betimes. Don't I have a cottage door open beside me? My friend, future lover and husband… listen to me. You were my help-meet all along, in that the object of your abandoned eyes led on to me. This proved not to be an exercise in contingency, no, but the magnetism of Robert Graves' *White Goddess* delivered you to me. Quickly, fasten yourself to the complexity of my dreams! Look at this poniard which is strapped next to my thigh by a thread of transparent gold. Do you detect its faintness now (?); especially when it's akin to a bronzed leg pulsating underneath."

Mezzanine Spratt: "Who are you?"

Tanith Carpentier: "May you stare at my breath-taking beauty, stranger! Let's consider it to be an example of Cleopatra's innocence – when taken together with a Grecian dome, at once amber to its nectar, plus some pale blue lips. They must be aflame with passion. Haven't I used a golden or fluorescent eye-shadow… one that was just smeared on such basilisk reaches? Can you detect their lust? Doesn't the hair-do – merely pleated in its peroxide magnificence – register *Lulu*… particularly as regards a certain White case of dreadlocks? You know of her Stygian vaultedness or white 'Rastafarianism'? She was the main character or nymphomaniac loadstar in Alban Berg's opera. But, to reverse a spell, my armour bears about it Macha's trace… that is: the female crone in Celtic mythology. All of this takes place at a time where all revere her next to a raven's tracery."

Mezzanine Spratt: "Where are we?"

Tanith Carpentier: "Do your dreams fail to instruct those frontal lobes in Gray's *Anatomy*; at least according to which such co-ordinates are traced? Wayward man, you've been drawn towards a magnet that's concealed under some chlorinated paper. Wherein Michael Farraday's postulates were signed off in terms of ferrous filings and their electro-magnetism.
++

Loving one, my game of snakes and ladders has led you to a sorcerer's village. Here magic reigns supreme without any stint, brook or surcease. It comes to be regarded as untrammelled (you see). Perhaps it would do you good to think of yourself as a character trapped in Dennis Wheatley's semiotic or in a novel like *The Satanist*… for example. How can one gain access to this hamlet, you ask? Why, it comes about on wild and stormy nights – if we might quote Bulwer Lytton. It is at such a moment that strangers or outsiders then find the gate to a forbidden cosmogony. Do you navigate around a green door's metaphor (?); one which was made of wood and that conceals a garden behind its wall. (Whether one chooses to master it in diverse fictions… like those of Rosamund Lehmann or Arthur Machen, peremptorily). Remember now: you entered with free will or volition, and their Cerberus won't permit an exit! Too late: they know you're here. Like me, Mezzanine, my love, you entered accompanied by billowing even-song only never to leave."

Mezzanine Spratt: "Who are they?"

Tanith Carpentier: "Why, the Magicians…"

XIX

Biff and Boff, who were dressed in purple cowls and vestments, appear behind them. Whilst a motley collection of ill-assorted mountebanks follows on or aft, and they represent a choked-off sea. All of these denizens wear close-fitting gear – somewhat after the fashion of puppets in *Commedia dell'arte*. Each one of them comes to be reminiscent of Ensor's painting *Skeleton in a Mirror with Masks*. Basically then, this tableau relates to their peeling rind or magenta hoods.

+

Biff and Boff can scarcely conceal their sadism (thereafter). But where does Lord Talbot reside? "Harken, a delinquent has appeared amongst us. Are you aware – daughter of us all – that the circle's been transgressed by one who's known contamination… possibly via unhallowed meats? Could his hands and mouth have quaffed uncleanness or trotters; primarily by an example drawn from *The Road to Wigan Pier*? Might he be porcine; at least in those terms which are available within a novel labelled *The Pork Butcher*? Our matzos aren't kosher (withal). No matter: you won't speak to us… leastwise, when it comes to negotiating the zip we've fastened over your faces. HA! HA! HA! HA! HA! HA! HA! HA! Let's also adjust to the following channel…"

Lord Talbot has Biff and Boff smeared across his features. "Leaven this bread of ecstasy, my fellow sprites! For our ambulance had trundled off into a sense of transparent gloom. Now we realise the chance to seize upon unhallowed rites! Again, a beam split from its enclosure – even though the red light atop the ambulance didn't flicker at all. It decomposed to a scarlet residue under the trees or next to a vehicle's blue. Needless to say, Biff injected Mezzanine with a narcotic in order to keep him hopeless and docile. Do you visualise it? A gothic imprimatur captured this… while Biff's face snarled in rapture; it milked its sapphire tint and came surrounded by a verdant cape. His teeth grinned on in a gorilla-like manner from inside those incisors; especially when congruent to a reptile's masking-up. A dull, Imperial purple reflected an absent glow thereafter. 'Why take such measures?', hissed Mezzanine Spratt. 'It's the avoidance of discord or the merry-go-round of an uncertain wake. A kitchen-sink drama by John Bratby (it may well be) which gives the lie to your position. It happens to be hopeless…', hinted or chortled Boff. During all this period he failed to conceal a chuckle or a stentorian guffaw. Does it need to be conceded – given a sun-dial's gloom?"

XX

Biff and Boff rise before us again… plus the briefest residue of a corn-dolly. It burns up abreast of you and reflects the naked light (thereby). Could it be stacked up or cantilevered in its maximum style? Surely its baroque magnificence hungered for such a flame?

+

"HA! HA! HA! HA! HA! HA! HA! HA! Let's imbibe the following mineral water… even if it's negative to the taste. May it recall a tableau or a dividend where shaven-headed troopers stand muster? They continue to sit in serried rows, ranks or phalanxes. Do you comprehend it all? Whereupon a three-pronged utensil is manoeuvred about (somewhat busily) and it travels along a gruel's cube if only to descend thereon. A crunch or a thud then occurs. Wasn't there that scene in Anthony Burgess' *The Wanting Seed*, a science fiction drama, where cannibalism takes place in cans marked 'munch'? (Note: it happens to be a pun on the German word for Man). Likewise, these youths' faces look serene or untroubled before a day's ordeals. Certainly, these ephebes betoken a squad of marines or commandos rather than bohemians. On closer inspection one of them delineates Mezzanine's features or carapace – albeit in silhouette. Suddenly a voice cracks out: 'Desist from consumption… don't eat it, Spratt. Each cube has to be rancid beyond salience. It contains brain-drain chemicals which are destined to chill one's factors.' But who advances such a warning? Why, it must be a middle-aged Biff who's leavened to a corse and flying on an electric bath-chair. (A seating arrangement that's accompanied with much gadgetry). He also appears invisible to those myrmidons roundabout. They carry on regardless of all help or assistance; and yet our phantom still speaks. 'You'll need every aspect of your faculties, my boy. Clear up and control the mind's plenitude --- it belongs to you!' A little further in we notice whether Biff's face comes blue-covered or tinted, and a sort of spherical emblem was emblazoned across it. It covers half of the available skin. He then pointed at Mezzanine with an arching finger or digit, and a gauntlet enclosed its development. Didn't his mother ever tell him it's rude to point? To which Spratt responded by saying: "Shut up! By Ymir, silence is golden in its plenitude or terms.' Even though – in response to his gesture – his immediate cohort sees nothing remiss. All remains invisible to them and they look about each other in perplexity. 'There he goes again', says one of their number. 'Has he developed a fetish for ranting against the air? Does he discern one's ether to be choc full of daemons – like in a Hieronymous Bosch painting?' Mezzanine responded by refusing to answer any of them. He continued to stare onwards and outwards moodily. Perhaps, in a manner put forward by Colin Forbes in *The Endless Game*, he realises the precious nature of silence. Shall he even ask for John Cage's endorsement at a later date…? But, even at a tender age, Spratt felt himself to be unburdened by a gadfly voice."

XXI

Tanith Carpentier finds herself beholden to a siren inside her suitor's mind. "Hold on now, lover. They may come for you aslant of Breughel's wasteland, but there's no need to fear. Since courage fastens to its own regard… especially across such a barren acreage. Do you remember a dream's forbidden values? Wherein a recruit is led towards a punishment squad that's situated on a sandy plain (now). It proves to be adjacent to a modernist structure; itself reminiscent of one of Mies van der Rohe's. Can't you recapture Ayn Rand's *The Fountainhead*; at least when seen through a grisaille or its angularity? No matter, my eye-candy. For this dimension depicts a phalanx in serried rows or about to administer some discipline. It involves 'running the gauntlet' after a Rugby custom like quad-flogging, for instance. Yet these young troopers array themselves around a miscreant or varmint (here), and they're eager to strike. Each one drew on a reflex's baton in order to run through a comrade readily; (i.e., one of their number who hadn't made the grade). 'We'll tighten you up, my weakling', suggests a smirking thugee. Another remarks thus: 'let's rifle him with a halbert, or even a combined spear and battle-axe.' 'Enough talk', wheedles a third, 'I'm anxious to beat upon savoury meats.' To which a younger Mezzanine Spratt responds: 'you boneless larvae… I despise you all. Go on and take your kicks – you wretches and their spawn.' 'AAAAGGHH!', they all cry in unison. 'Prevail upon him not to pass – certainly in terms of an oblivion's posting. Yes sir…' 'Make away, my fellow knaves, and remove your shoulders from those bladed bones. I want to crack open those legs so as to execute the marrow within. Aha(!), just look at this ventriloquist's orbs and their necessary spiralling. Have I fixed him to the workbench by placing a pin through a beetle, thereby?'"

Simultaneously though, doesn't such a thunder flash resemble an early Punch & Judy? A scenario wherein Punch emerges from behind a purple cloak. May Sir Harrison Birtwhistle's atonality accord with this swazzle or its psychic attributes? After all – only Mezzanine stood outside a booth on the shingle or its sound. For there weren't any children to respond to our *Grand Guignol's* 'blood and thunder'. Truly, the child within us requires violent emotions or spleen – particularly when set off against an absolute moral code. Yet metaphysical objectivism can't really compete with a wall of dolls when they're laid out by Waldo Lanchester, photographically speaking. Do we respond to their grins, revolving eyes, sinister mien and *papier mache* heads? Also, let's never mind a bestiary's pomegranates… for these were lost around its ovoid touch and hachures. Nor do they look like Marion Manson!

XXII

Yet these turquoise-clad mages command elemental tones or lays, such as flickering flames or an Indian rope-trick. "Up lasso", they proclaim to various inanimate objects… "Go to the outsider and bind him fast, or hand and foot."

Mezzanine Spratt: "What is this?"

Biff and Boff: "It remains our rendition of a full metal-jacket, stranger. Have you recognised the labyrinthine quality of so many dreams? A drama within which you savour a miasma – always delivered headless and redolent of Punch's gibbet (plus a cranium in a box). Doesn't such a headsman indicate sensory panic? Necessarily so, since water and fire are both symbols of a 'heretic' world in Alchemy! Furthermore, any adventures like these take note of your light-heartedness… given that Tanith Carpentier walks away from Mezzanine, who's held captive in a bath with various hippogriffs on every corner. Certainly she stalked on velvet green *avec* the latter twisting and turning on piles, each one Gothic to this last… They rose up out of a tessellated floor; together with the exhibition of many victims who were lassoed above. Might these cadavers embody a 'plastinate' by Professor Gunter von Hagens, the anatomist? Still, a pink embrasure filled the screen *a la* von Stroheim's flickerings… or their monstrous and composite body. Again, this was not to mention those blue friezes which were perfectly symmetrical and gave a mesmerism to one's floor-sheen. In its arithmetic, then, this parquet recalled a mosaic or alternatively a *lapis* drawn from Islamic art. Behind her hyacinth a dioxaxine purple swept away which showed Biff in silhouette. While those reptilian fancies – themselves born of mystification – began to shower Mezzanine with sulphur. He lay (for his part) chained to the inside of this vessel within which such toads vomited their fancy!

+

Do they at once essay creatures in Hieronymous Bosch's *The Temptation of Saint Anthony*? For here, they besport themselves within alabaster or a new roof. Yet – on occasion – a snout-faced creature who is dressed in black, porcine or sallow, and with a mandolin or lute… why, 'he' crosses a threshold between life and death. Isn't that the case? *L'homme propose et Dieu dispose…* Moreover, what about the owl which perches on his scalp? Because all polycephalous spectres come to a point where they recommend this. Again, each figurine was maimed in its quietude and it lay adjacent to a machine that looks on indifferently, or alters its trajectory. May sepulchral gloom play a part herein? Further, why does a virgin over-straddle the saint by proffering a dish of Holy Water? In comparison to which, various owls make hay with arrested purity before an oneiric defeat. Yes… these mediums sought to lift a veil on the next life; if only to cast a chiaroscuro upon twilight or its semblance. Do you detect any sundry import? Since this perverseness renders itself aloof with distant shadows or halves; themselves shrunken or betokening dwarves. All in all, they mushroom out as Grotesques – thence occurring on the margins of manuscripts or bewildering us in their illumination. Are they basically a bygone age's incunabula?"

XXIII

Mezzanine Spratt: "My form has concocted a rope or its step-ladder; the levitation of which surrounds me from every side. It holds me bitterly in such an entreaty. Furthermore, these mages think that they've bound me hand and foot… but Tanith stands beside me now. She leans against my blue-garbed body… so the weight of her hand might conceal something. It (whatever its nature) writhes adjacent to her scarlet dress."

Meanwhile, the purple-clad magicians gather in a hemicycle around their 'victims'. A strange hum comes up from their serried mouths (betimes). For a brief moment it embodies a Greek chorus which is nearly always pursuant to tragedy.

Doesn't such an assemblage consist of old men in masks from two-and-a-half millennia ago? Moreover, each and every one of them fails to put forward a different view, collectively speaking. *Lex talionis*… can a law of retribution suffice?

Biff and Boff refer to their stuffed arm-pits (anonymously): "Look onwards from this, the two of you! Since to one side of Saint Anthony's demon – when accustomed to its left – a rival figure emerges. It was a cripple – otherwise locked into self-trespassing – and carrying on servitude's burden. He shuffles outwards and onwards – albeit with one make-belief before a game and almost as if he can play a musical instrument. Could it be a harp or perhaps an Iberian guitar in the hands of one skilled to use it – like John Williams? Never mind – because these anthropomorphic types know their own kindred. Yet, irrespective of this, such wraiths maximise their circumference or leave nought to chance. Here flits half an owl… at least when filleted to smoke and glowering across an engagement's tempera. It rescues its plinth in a manner which mocks a game of skill. This proceeds on a neighbouring table that's circular in form. Various biomorphic tents whisk about – some are part vegetal in aspect; while others track a beetle to its lair. Don't we register it in the dream which this narrative has been plagued with?

+

Again, a head whirled around Mezzanine and Tanith with an elongated snout. It came to be blinded by its ice or snow, and this death-mask laughed maniacally across some lace net-curtains. Do you recall whether Tanith is a moon goddess from Carthage? But – in reality – it just intimated Bedlam or Hans Prinzhorn's *The Art of the Insane*; at least after Gaius Cibber's statues reaching out for one afore. These gigantic jaws sprawled over in a lop-sided way. 'HA! HA! HA! HA! HA! HA! HA! HA! HA! HA! HA! HA! HA! HA! HA! HA!', they roared.

+

Still and all, her skull has been picked up and it spat fire from woefully green irises. In point of fact, her orb floats up via depths of red and brown… but what did she have wedged between her lips other than a scarab? An insect that's crawled there primarily in one's imagination. For haven't you heard whether every *beetle draws a sting*, or not? Of what else abounds, perchance (?); why, it's merely an unconscious revelation…

+

Because once the girl known as Tanith wanders abroad with those magicians… they cut off her head with a mock-guillotine! This device was originally concealed behind a hillock which proves russet in its hue. Whilst our homunculus or *invunche* drains the gore from her severed neck into a porcelain bowl. Mightn't it have been made from spode china (?); or a reflex on one's distaff side? Even so: she remains alive --- in spite of all."

XXIV

Tanith speaks now and her irises were brightly lit up – so as to fill the available sockets. No astigmatism fails to communicate a story like this (you see).

Tanith Carpentier: "One's head-chicken's sprout is off and you're even free to make a wish. Where has all of this blood come from (?); and it's reminiscent of the first stages of an infant's birth. Ugh! Yonder pot contains those innards which belaboured one's insides – certainly prior to any relief. What purpose do one's intestines have when confronted with the knife? A poniard too far, one feels… yes, my spirituality makes free to float like a bird that's unburdening its aura. But truly, any impermanence must mark time… for my sureness finds its sacrifice aslant a miracle or forlorn of all tissue. My head was off – you see – and it bounces after a ball with its green-eyes distended. A scene where the colour of a scalp remains pearlescent or it rides its luck, and it comes to be surrounded by rose's penumbra. All I can manage by way of a shout is: 'UGGHH…glug-glug-glug!' Never mind, since one's rootedness in the ground has to be an absence of legs… no matter how prior.

Perhaps now, my rind can be picked up by Biff – especially when next to a stalk or its root of the brightest yellow?"

Mezzanine, if still pursuant to a Punchman's swazzle: "You mustn't forget the reproach of 'Saint Anthony's temptation'! A painting wherein the saint wears a cowl next to his grace and irrespective of any loucheness. Do you realise the solace that's afoot? For one larceny exists within a sow's recognition or in terms of a grey eminence which lists blackly. He approaches Saint Anthony sideways-on; and yet remains undefeated by silence. Don't you recognise its similarity to a copperhead (?); namely, the most poisonous snake on the north american mainland. Or alternatively, this summoned up a pulp fiction character who's been unlicensed by Keneth Robeson. May it comprehend a magic camera, thereby? Because this sloth or gut-wrench looms up from the side; whereas his movements were ungainly and resembled a hippy's over-drive... or a beatnik's gait. Could this possibly deliver up Kerouac's desolation angels (?); never mind the call of Pynchon's 'Lot 49' or Acker's Algiers, sapphically speaking. Again, it slid into position with a banjo to hand, and do we detect a pistol in its belt or buttress? Let's see: this pig-man zig-zagged towards our church father who had black satin accompanying his *Facial Justice*. Wasn't the latter an anti-socialist novel by L.P. Hartley (?); and didn't such a troubadour make an unlikely exorcist?"

XXV

Our black magicians – when garbed in a grey lotus – stood around their fire-storm. Certainly, Tanith's head was off and her golden eyes glinted in the dust. Wasn't this a distillation coming up for air amid a watery grave? Still, these liquids have a brown streak shot through their centre. Might it encode an ochre tint (?); particularly when captured by its loss or swirling within opaque depths. Anyway – in comparison to the above – Tanith's severance found itself supported; while those orbs let loose a stream by way of a rivulet or its spasm... and in terms of salty tears. By the way, didn't Iris Murdoch write a novel called *A Severed Head*?

+

Carpentier's skull then comes to embody a brush-stroke; albeit plus an earthy sediment. Were her orbs open to a silent or silver screen, and in comparison to her lush hair? Does one sense its unforgiveness, now? A scenario where her arms loom up in a stupor – so as to master the adamantine quality of those glass-eyes! Much of which means that an M.R. James story comes into play; itself a variant on Sir Harrison Birtwhistle's opera *Punch and Judy*. (A work which has a libretto or vocal score by Stephen Pruslin). Nonetheless, the sluice-gates behind these dolls' eyes open up… primarily in order to carom a blue-green marble down into each socket. Irrespective of this, a beetle's antennae emerges from her mouth or cavern, and after an opal's impress. May such an insect mount its own tattoo (?); basically so as to summon up some woad. Look at it this way: a *Coleoptera* whose upper-wings have been converted to sunlight… why, it exits from her lips. It certainly pertains to one's mouth or tongue. Also, it seems to be a redundant gesture before the flying creature's mandibles. Every beetle draws a sting, don't you know?

XXVI

Tanith Carpentier: "I have a knife to hand which is hidden within my cloak's folds… and it's next to your sapphire mack. (She happened to be addressing Mezzanine Spratt in a low whisper at the time). For, like a Church-maiden who comforts Saint Anthony, I lean across a salvo and I'm undaunted over its closure. My dress – in circumstances such as these – trammels a delicate pink; particularly when taken together with a white shawl around my head. Don't I offer sweet-meats or a watery compendium (?); at least in terms of a God in the Bowl."

Biff and Boff exist some way off. They are surrounded by lesser Grand Masters and look like members of British Israel. "Surprisingly, we are ahead of you or at our thinking's discretion, my dear. Because daemonic presences are merely an entreaty's tad-pole. Given this, one crippled lutanist approaches a reddened hearth (thereby). Mightn't he be playing his stick forlornly (?); or otherwise proving oblivious to all else? He came accompanied by a carnival's dog; the former a mutt who wears a wine-coloured hood about his cheeks. Do you retain a regard for these facts? When we consider that those reptiles which do so, Tanith, move eastwards from the west to the accompaniment of a chestnut hue. It settles, this latter dispensation, upon chocolate: i.e., a chiaroscuro shot through with fire and akin to red egg-tempera. But still these hog-heads or heresiarchs move closer… and all the while they are composing that lute music which spoke of an alchemist's 'bridal chamber'. Yess-ss-ss."

(Note: British Israel is a Gentilist and supremacist cult).
Tanith Carpentier: "Tell me, coven of warlocks, what befell my head in another dimension or space, and after it had been severed from its trunk?"

Those male witches who are gathered in conclave can only sneer in reply: "Why don't you use your imagination, girl?"

For what fate opens up – when pursuant to a Death's-head – can only be this volute… in which, *mutatis mutandis*, the knife, spear, arrow, sword and axe all make their appearance. They happen to be assorted emblems of Alchemical fire and each helps to feed its furnace. Do us a favour – why don't you? By virtue of the fact that this head swivels free from its corse; if only to manoeuvre beyond a night-time's borders. Are you brave enough to see it? Further, this plastinate found itself linked to such a balustrade, contained, as it was, within some plexiglass. Can one remember a character known as Doctor Sun from a graphic novel of yesteryear? Never mind: since her cranium whips around quickly, and it caroms like a billiard or snooker ball with a sigil on its tongue. It indicates a beetle's impress… resultantly. At the same time as this, my friend, any attempt to grasp her dome causes it to rear up like a fun-fair's device. Doesn't it career about? She can even travel across the floor without aid – especially if it happens to be shiny or translucent, and rather like sand after a dose of nuclear fusion. Yes indeed, this is radioactively speaking… even though such a truckle-bed recalls one of those cripples who were drawn by Grosz, the expressionist, and made use of by Brecht. (It also relates to the Boer War from 1899-1902, in light of an updated *Beggars' Opera*). Finally, Tanith's decapitation veers off with much *élan*; if only for its cage to become clamped to a rocket. It soars into outer space and follows a projectile's ellipse/eclipse. Thereafter, and rather like one of NASA's shuttles, it was blown to smithereens in the Milky Way.

XXVII

Tanith Carpentier: "Quick, your hands are free, thanks to my knife's insistence. Let's run for your car which exists at the heart of a square in this hamlet… it is just like Port Meirion in Patrick McGoohan's *The Prisoner*. Nothing will stop us – irrespective of those magicians who stand guard next to your convertible. Move – my trampoline – make haste… get out; we must cross the threshold from one reality into another one."

Mezzanine Spratt: "Now that I've found you, I'm not going without you."

Tanith Carpentier: "Darling, help grant me a courage comparable to your own. With you beside me, all last vestiges of fear become stripped from me!"

The mages Biff and Boff are possibly screeching this for the last time. "STOP… don't pass towards such a tunnel of flame! We command you to desist!" <<<This occurs slightly afore her rush to the car; a feat which is aided and abetted by Mezzanine.>>>
++

OPERATION RE-WIND: *if we were to begin again…*

I

Which road should one take through life; at once immature to its particular stillness? For Mezzanine Spratt lay slumped in his convertible's seat, red in colour, with heavy rain beating on his windscreen above the wipers. But one's mind lay elsewhere; irrespective of those gloved hands that gripped the wheel. He should have taken a previous turn; itself locked in the implementation of its wood… and way back there in an inky diaspora.

Mezzanine Spratt: "A parepraxis wanders abroad in terms of a free-flowing bio-cast. Can one credit it? Since one fork in this road doesn't prepare me for an exclusion, given the toucan which is mirrored in turquoise and who rests on a tropical branch. Various figures gather below in vegetation's clearing; they are roundabout, spectral and seen in microscopic size. Let them waste themselves in illusion or by wrestling a breach; a factor which leaves them unprepared for a biological misfit. He looms up later. It stands head-to-toe in these leaves; the latter being sore in its study of such violence. Any head-dress so worn derives from the sward; it exists as a deluge of humus hanging down. It also configures its own wake --- at least in terms of like carrion. Do you interpret this matter differently? Each one of us addresses a configuration on the sly; a distribution of identity that occasionally slips over into phantasm. Our contribution also comes minus a semblance of living bark; the former enlivened to a pitch or sliver. Now isn't this altogether necessary? For a bat flits away from us in Bram Stoker's chronicle; it was held inside a dark tumbrel and relished the closing out of one enemy too far. Such a tunnel proved to be very deep; it even came to be separated from such a funnel by one's entreaty. Its abundant roots found themselves inflected with herbs. Such a string-fellow bellyaches against one's sky; in a way that's lost on this particular occasion. Or – alternatively speaking – these fronds curl over a skeleton which is accompanied by so many weeds. Didn't the Bible call them *tares*? He raced on or became tied fast to a new oblivion, and he lived only for the Green. Down into this mud one's spectrum remained enclosed; or it breathed out through pores in the earth – no matter how sovran. A snake moves silently; it just slithers now over the ground without shedding any skin. (This was irrespective of how luckless it could otherwise be!) Yet a bilious caution fills these vagaries – somewhat emptily. Wasn't there a post-situationist magazine in the 'eighties called *Vague*? Regardless of this: a magenta inundation speckles the sky; it essentially rises towards one's gait – together with a gathering of crows who thrust their momentum outwards. Sure enough, the blinding of this sun is caused by beating wings – each one of which was given as a token to its saviour. Throughout the gathering or purple gloom, however, only a total sense of blackness can retrieve its grandeur. It does not circle merely, but sweeps up apace in order to close out the storm.

+

A sequence of abandonment closes down the dial. It moves inwards (as a consequence) in order to catapult a sunny measure towards its rim. One, two, three, four and five minutes elapse; while a dot or its attendant speck mounts towards a chaotic and confused state. It continues to run on and thereby fills the darkness with its pink globule. May it be a sloth creature or taxidermic relic – like one of Doctor Moreau's vivisections? Who knows? Yet it dances upon a pin-head which is occasioned by swathes of emerald (rather bluntly), but he or 'it' runs backwards with a hand behind its bank. Is this head reversed or Bishop-like in its diagonal movement… while agonising over such a source? Still, on it galloped forsooth… albeit with a yellow loin-clout surrounding its bravery or otherwise costumed to a fight. Out its hands reached and spittle daubed its past; at a time when craniums were twinned base-about-apex (no matter how redundantly). Does this resemble the scene – when kindled to diabolical possession – in Peter Blatty's *The Exorcist*? Never mind: since one cranium can only manufacture a semblance within identity, even when scared over this origin or momentarily magisterial… possibly so. It runs into me screaming 'AAAAGGGHHHH!'; *avec* a litany of sputum running from his teeth. It happens to be Boff. Do we see the bravery of this adult babe (thereafter)? No way… For a hand reaches out to crush my vertebrae or spine, and it basically grabbed me about the face… as it squeezes itself unto death (sufficiently so). I am abreast of such an essence; at least being riven or graven to a kaleidoscope of liquid orange. Are my features screeching over into each other (most effectively); and do they deliver their sound by way of an abstract expressionist medley? Can each of us detect another's advent? Hardly… because this squashed remnant catapults its compass into red, primarily by dint of anger or its copper-bottom – never mind such silent screeds. Has the tone-poem of this crust cried out (?); or become abreast of a motor… and is it really adjusted to haemoglobin? I cry out so as to afford some necessary relief. My mind then kneads in the direction of a silvery haze; at once bathed in *lapus lazuli* and growing darker… It falls between one's pages (rather necessarily); as it proves to be lifted out beyond the self. Ever so powerfully (then)… Oughtn't I to have fallen asleep in this way (?); thereby slumping across a car's steering-wheel. Surely a way out of this nightmare lies in witnessing sleep's absence…?"

II

Tanith Carpentier: "He dozes – while I dream… the latter occasioned by those yearnings for love inside me. Am I his phantom play-thing (?); or *vice versa*? No matter: are we to work the prey of our desires, even if we fall out of consciousness? Behind me this mental thicket waxes dark green – despite a misunderstanding which occurs with some grey. But perhaps it's best to wait (?), or to sense the skull beneath the skin in an Elisabethan's words? Decidedly so – my teeth happen to be the most arresting feature: all of them running out of account and even staring with orb-like eyes… or just defending each nakedness in its verdure. Don't you know that a new Medusa must be an expert in topiary? Assuredly, I race into such greenery with my arms flailing – the one assertively bitten to the bone; while the other casts specks of starlight around me. Each particle pulsates like a flexing atom – even though it finds itself griddled to the paw: in a situation where it barely substitutes for these available eyes. Soon little was left of it all, at least in its afforded silhouette, save a rising filter twice over: and each and every one of them pondered on this device. Yet soon one is connected to the antechamber of a dark room, a space which sounds very quiet and was filled by a rectangular echo. May it be pretensions of John Cage's music to fill up a sombre zone like this? Since minimalism retreats from its serried articulation (thereby)? Furthermore, will anyone feel free enough to assess the planes of Shaker furniture?"

Biff and Boff choose to persevere as our magicians. (Have they opened up the back of Spratt's head; if only to look in through a glass panel, metaphorically? Yes, our answer comes to us in golden tones; especially in terms of those hanging apples).

"This figure floats within a membrane of emerald; it circles down with each limb separate from one another… and bursting from its quartered bounds. He dives within an amniotic fluid; the former being blue to one's taste or wild… While various masses of plant-life seem to be growing up within it, a few of them might be sentient or trading blow for blow. A large foetal off-break sits with an imbalance in its silence; it belabours the point and comes to be held in pink. But still he spirals down within an eddy or its fall; and 'he' occasionally draws up towards him the raptures of our deep. Whereas great cells grow out of each other betimes; they are abundantly cancerous, mock-red or swelling before each doom. Every one contains within it the crystalline folly of a new abstraction; a factor that's basically deviant to this last – but which grows apace by hyperbole. It cascades ever onwards, do you notice it? Since such spheroid skulls as these mount agape;

nor do they merely witness one's Tyburn tree or siphon it off into a play-station (thereafter). Above us these tides turn in a maelstrom or its immensity; and they beckon beyond us towards the grave… Yet they remain alone; if somewhat isolated. 'Can I hurl myself forwards?', he asks… at a time when he's just joined to this rupture, but not by any steadfast indent. Hold on! For blue bubbles move around his cortex and brain, if only to festoon an eye-ball: itself brought up sharp and centring on the iris. It looms out against a possibly misshapen scarlet or swells to a fitting cure – primarily so as to reveal a black dot at the heart of this couplet. Let's sneak up close to the rim of such a cornea… the latter festooned at an eye-ball's heart. Don't we really discern a blinding light here (?); one which looks expectant in its glow (essentially). Further, it contrives to fill up one's mental screen or dish – like in Michael Powell's film *Peeping Tom*. Wherein the rich go forward to die or bake out such a prospect; and they see the whole zodiac in an instant while listing to a negative colour. Never trust these results, my friend, because a refulgent burst fills one's screen (albeit momentarily).

III

Mezzanine Spratt: "Again we find a spectrum in this darkness – one that's sent listening to any sound and without a blunt beacon further off… Even though such a glow-worm flickers *avec* the alacrity of one of Derby's lights. (This is Wright of Derby, the painter of the industrial revolution – do you recall?) To be sure: a blue sweep-stake grows up behind us; whereas its penumbra illuminates the whole… As two figures amble forward with each of them withering to a torch in its light – plus the reverse archaeology of caves growing all around them. May it be an opposite chasm of non-identity (?); one which feasts on this rapture underground, and that signals off at various levels *avec* some light green oxide… together with prism violet and Prussian blue. Does she embody – at this moment in the proceedings – a western punk *per se* (?); or the innermost matrix of Siouxie Sioux and *the Slits*? Was Ambrose Bierce right in his reckoning;

primarily in terms of her Mohican shawl or its withering haze? But what of Tanith's eyes, though? They were azure or deepening to purple, even if maddened and looking in… no doubt. Yet again – each of them swayed to its course like a marble: with either orb sovereign in its hate or otherwise caught out… It also proved to be capable of a sly interlude, an *aporia* in being; one which can be interpreted later on through mirrors. Sideways-on or refracted they are – whilst being urgently mystified over a source; and they're often unkind… despite penetrating these leathery shadows under a tousle of flickering flame. Isn't it true that punks lit up their hair – when all aglow – like human cockatoos? Whereas one fact escaped their attention and this was – amid American and Australian slang – that the word means hustler, mountebank, beseecher, even moral whore… Wherein a black execution or nihilism closes in around them; if only to reveal this truth."

IV

Biff and Boff dwell on a triumphant accomplice, if only in their dreams. "Let's look at a resounding distaff, my friends. For an eye rears out of a quadrant of self. It has blood specked around its circumference – the former being rheum red and travelling to its source, or finding itself delivered within the refraction of a camera's instant. Yes… are these configurations falling away in a curving arc thereby? Most assuredly… *quod* Mezzanine Spratt has arrived. He lies within a circle of ochre or finds himself reflected in its vice, and it's fairly cracked over the impermanence of concrete… nor need it be adult in its way-station. Various geographical features become pronounced… since horror's charm is the sweetest and most moral of traps. Again now, Spratt finds himself chained to a lathersome instant; primarily by way of a wall, altogether silted over, and ignoring both fate and fortune. It stares up at a carriage of cerulean blue… if only to be surrounded by demons. They were modelled after a mediaeval *Book of Hours* (or some other bestiary). Similarly, these creatures loll around a basin's incline – whether they choose to be hippogriffs, Aztecs or hyper-tensioned extras. Nor can we move towards such a gap in our fortunes; at least without measuring the cost. They squat upon Gothic *facades* or stones; each within a luxuriant purview… and across this balustrade lies an insect's shadow. It – the beetle – stains the shape or format of a gigantic tattoo. Do you justify it thus? It may be in woad or code, but nothing really matters save its name. It happens to be a *Mecynorrhina Polyphemus* from Congo Zaire – especially when labelled to its source (however appropriately). Doesn't it prove to be multiple across its hump-backed course? Can it make any difference to those gathered roundabouts? May it cross various planes of identity? Most particularly… when a beetle's hint draws down the sting of its conscience – albeit in reverse!"

V

Mezzanine Spratt is basically able to narrate his prologue because of an absence of verses. "Oh yes, Spratt lies within a circular distemper; it's overly finished but otherwise rich in phosphorous… Given their provender, one was able to locate chains behind his hands. While the sand aslant his back waxes yellow, possibly mysterious, or akin to an earthquake's aftermath. Still, the reptilian entities around him gibber – all of them about to take part in the most unholy of rites! Might one notice its abundance or fissures? Above him the figure of Biff glowers down upon his shadow… it's again compacted to a rage of non-identity. His essential characteristics were as follows: (one) an enormous staff made of black teak; (two) the amplitude of a mortal's arm at its end. It also recalls a mild distemper in its claret; at least *via* small skulls and faces attached to its livery… But yet, the blood-sodden eyes of those who are to perish face defeat; an intent that's fused together with their entrails. *Avaunt thee*! Next to him stands Boff with his head on backwards; it exists inside the trunk; i.e., as a mask fixed to its aspidistra. It certainly flows away towards an onset of gold. This face also dances abreast of a lustrous grin; it subsists amid a vista of deranged pink. Truly, this has to remember Boff's nemesis –

what with the cranium reversed out or put on back to front, by way of completion. It spreads out – likewise – across too wide a field of hate, at least in terms of extending or balanced margarine. You see? In any event, our picture must be finished by virtue of a savoury run… in relation to this, Biff wears an orange robe up to a hooded top. It makes leave to support a head-dress; and does he sport a beard as well?

+

Anyway, this undoubted inclination or resolve had to spend itself – if it doesn't reconnoitre an observance outside time. Nonetheless, such a tapestry of wills may summon up a painting by Max Beckmann. Surely it was known as *Perseus* (?); a picture that followed a right-hand wing or triptych. A visualisation of blondeness is kept apparent – in which both main characters inhabit a cage. A devastation of lines and stirrups lies about, even though the territory indicates a passion for green and orange. But what of this bird (?) – one that's located to the east, (betimes), or sporting a human head over a vermillion torso. Might it be pecking at the entrails of its own soul? By any reckoning, such a vulture looks sour or lugubrious, even other-worldly and avuncular… if incomplete without palsy. Old Father Time (Biff) rests thereupon – with his claws reckoning to scratch a crook or its bark. Yet what will he be thinking or absorbing (?) under those thick brows of reverse piety…"

VI

The voice of Tanith Carpentier is held in suspended animation – despite the fact that she may not be there. "A green sward swirls before these eyes' temptation – themselves circling in a hybrid density. It can well reach the onset of these open graves. Has she approached the edge; or an extremity of its redemptive pain? Anyway, the master mage known as Biff gazes down on his captive or prey. Observe this, my fellows… for both eyes are red and spectral in their import – especially when occasioning a run down a face's scorbutic texture. It merely meets up in a brief pointillism of beard. Is it clear? Yes, Biff's crown clothes itself *avec* a filament of rags; each one wound around the cranium like a winding-sheet… and near to a salutary death. Yet ossuaries are unforgiving; they look to the future through an analysis of past selves! Each one of them is not necessarily codified in glory. A ring in the left nostril makes play with Ionescu, in that it gestures to its own gallery's accomplishment. Let's just listen to a pattern of demons under their hooves… May we give him utterance – primarily in a voice which enjoins water dripping off a stalactite in a cave? Be it (netherwise) so deeply underground…"

Biff – plus an acorn growing out of his aphrodisiac… Shall it ever retrieve the will of a lion? "Mezzanine… Mezzanine… Mezzanine… Welcome to a hearth of outright slaughter! You are amongst enemies now. We shall show you no mercy – irrespective of those lizards climbing up the stalks in front of one. These configurations have limned themselves across yon face; at once congealed though it be. See here… are you aware of an expanse of temperature running away from you… out towards those purple constellations within the mind? --- Take this down or notate it freely, will you? Mezzanine Spratt, you find yourself trapped within concentric circles or spirals… each one addressing a new compartment. Abreast of this temple an egg exists; it's hale and hearty over an inheritance (accordingly). Yes… even such cliffs or trees succumb to abandoned shapes; now that one's passed beyond them. Any road up, I can sense a subtle careering in your dreams, as it hurls itself over – screaming all the while. *Touche*! Can each mask reckon to a salutary bloodbath over form? Wherein Ensor's transliterations think laterally or in a curve… particularly when pregnant and caterwauling.

+

Suddenly her stockinged legs were above him, thence providing a momentary significance to these proceedings. Weren't they mesh tights or otherwise fish-net (?), with a pink residue of flesh fading into a turquoise awakening."

VII
Mezzanine Spratt: "You're here to gloat, then?"

Tanith Carpentier: "Gloating remains the sacrifice of a victim which doesn't know its glory."

Mezzanine Spratt: "I wonder if you've the stomach for an enabling discharge."

Tanith Carpentier: "Quiet… the rain is coming down on the inside of your skull. If you remain silent for a moment, you'll hear it."

Mezzanine Spratt: "Wretch, no wonder man can never trust woman since the Garden of Eden! Nothing prelapsarian may rest enough for an adder to make its way up your leg (effectively)."

Tanith Carpentier: "Flattery cuts no ice with those who are accustomed to seeing a skull in one's picture. It's autobiographical, you see. Do you remember the elongated Golgotha which breaks up the flow of Holbein's *The Ambassadors*, replete with a velvet green betwixt?"

Mezzanine Spratt: "All I can recall to memory was that Savonarola's strictures about Renaissance painting were right. For Botticelli's canvases are impregnated with a pagan lustre."

Tanith Carpentier: "Your nonchalance intrigues me. What force lies behind ebon lines drawn upon white, in terms of runic inscriptions which a skilled mind might read?"

Mezzanine Spratt: "That's easy… he's called Satan!"

VIII
He had driven off the road and almost into a ditch… yet still the rain thundered down relentlessly on his wind-shield. Wasn't this

so? Anyway, his head-light beams could hardly cut a swathe through the darkness beyond. Whereupon little black specks enlivened themselves on the glass pane across from his wheel, as gloved fingers grasped the steering instrument in front of him. While the water came down in sheets, nay torrents, which inundated the sides of his scarlet car and then passed away... down its available slip-stream. Furthermore, his head (primarily dressed in a trilby) almost dipped down so low that it came to press against the darkened pane. Slowly he decided to discontinue his journey onto the next city – where he dimly remembered his status as a travelling salesman. 'I can't go on', he thought, 'I'll have to stop here and take some rest when I can.' He then reversed the vehicle up, parking it next to a sodden bank of trees. Like a sluice-gate opening in reverse, he manoeuvred the car round so's he could park it effectively. Then, lowering the trilby's brow over his eyes, he settled down to forty winks. Soon Mezzanine Spratt, in his earthly incarnation, was fast asleep... but what a strange tableaux of dreams he has lately enjoyed!

Have those nightmares started up instead?

IX

Biff and Boff are together again at last: "A man can be as strong as he will allow himself to be... this is the first rule of magic. One does not even have to apprise oneself of Richard Cavendish's *The Black Arts* in order to know it. What congratulations we can offer each other, my brother-in-arms! Look, in this dimension, she stands above him with a coloured streamer in her hair... it cascades from such a promontory. May it swirl down from an accustomed baldness; itself riven by a knife's expectation? 'A poniard, my brother most drear?' 'You have assessed it correctly, sibling.' For the amplitude of a bare blade has to cover over the look of one hooliganism or another. It happens to be tonsured. Yes, the diffidence of such a fate must glance down – so as to cover a model's fortune. Grant this damage to the ascent of Man... since she stoops to retrieve a bag from the side-lines – when set against a sweeping backdrop of designer blue – and within which many a gargoyle squats. Do they represent the tale-end of an eighteenth century draughtsman's contract? Steady now… because Tanith holds up a brown canvas sack in front of her. It comes to our attention in a tatty manner, bursting at the seams, and it remains corded at the top by a length of tarred rope. What could it possibly be? Well… Mezzanine stares up at her with a ready snarl upon his lips. One of his eyes has been closed by the impact of violence, and the man's aspen hair looks assaulted by wind or rain. Necessarily so, *quod* a funeral march of blood and gore ran laterally across Spratt's face – merely traversing its sloping field like a bishop in chess. Could this prove emblematic of an Anglo-Saxon rune? A proem in which a gaming-piece indicates a merry joust… all of it occurring amidst folk. Nonetheless, Spratt's teeth curdle over a realistic clench – while one eye gazes uppermost. It happens to be grey in its spectrum of colour; at least beyond the travesty of death. He investigates his feminine host's macabre intentions, thereby. Distantly, a pale inundation or daybreak passes over his jaw-line, even its lower partiality… And this is despite any residual cover in ultramarine.

+

What can be in this accursed bag? Well, she holds it delicately within ribbed fingers… in a manner that renders its bulk deceptive. May it really be about a basket-ball's sight and size? Moreover, it definitely concerns some carrion which can be jettisoned – out of all available stencils – and by way of one contrary limit. Assuredly, its cargo plummets down against a backdrop that was violently chromium oxide in its greenery. Further, the crepitation of its assault carries a fatalism with it… way out beyond these swards. A sickening thump occasions a rising or THWACK(!) – until one realises its existence as a human head… one which has been severed at the wrist."

X

Mezzanine Spratt: “whose skull might it be – primarily in terms of an estimation beyond the grave? Necessarily, it relates to my casing; albeit clothed in flesh and staring up at me with vacant orbs. Do you disinter such a prospect? Anyway, Tanith Carpentier left it lying there – essentially bagless – while she turned on her heel and strutted back towards the enclosure. Really? Might this vehicle for Gray’s *Anatomy* have come off… multi-dimensionally? An illustration (sic) where my head-piece just withers back, if delicately stitched, and in relation to a despondent body. Here again, the genuflexion of a muse is found wanting. Nor can we actually penetrate through the fog until we’ve perceived a head-in-a-box… On it floats – basically without entrails – and yet listening to a post. It swivels within a plexi-glass cage now; as it careers in one direction or another… whilst finding favour with none. Surely though, a needle in a hay-stack may find some refuge in fire… thence giving up the prospect of a Head’s separate quest? Given all of this: it is quite clear that a Jack-in-the-Box shall roll out many possibilities – as ‘it’ makes its way towards you on bitten linoleum. For the balance of probability remains pregnant with need, since our crown moves forward on a truckle-bed or tray. It consists of one of those boards with four wheels at every corner – just after a momentary passage or amplitude. Wasn’t it like a conveyance which cripples used to wear, preferably round their necks? Yet – on consideration – it revives one of those harsh memories or drafts by Grosz; the latter configuring maimed men in the Boer War (1899-1902). Didn’t it hint at Brecht’s use of Gay’s *Beggar’s Opera*? Still, the impact of these lines saw our head-stone speed onward – when renewed to a source of bliss – and definitely lost in sullen-eyed expectancy. Because its facial clefts are keenly etched – even blanked, balding or graven to an eldritch touch. His language also seems to trail off behind a bald pate, by virtue of a balloon and cast out of a Plexiglass dome… A token that finds itself scored with a dark silhouette – abreast of so much triviality.”

XI

Yet how goes it back on planet earth, with Mezzanine Spratt as a ready witness-statement? Firstly, he had begun to fall asleep in the car's front leather-seat. Again, rain continues to lash down on a glass above the dash-board. Shall there be, if you pardon its *scintilla*, an element of hail mixed in within it? To be sure: Spratt's trilby became more and more slumped down – as his head reclined with a greater lowness... particularly when set against the vanquished leather-cushions beneath. They bore about them an orange livery... during a period where the man's hat stooped towards a plastic steering-wheel. Dun-coated it was, yet Mezzanine seems to dwell on his life's presumed loneliness, without either a wife or a partner to help things along. Zzzzzzzzzzz... He went on sleeping – with just those ricocheting pellets of water for company. Suddenly his scalp bobbed up; it's occasionally pursuant to a stray sheet of lightning that lit up the night-sky. Must he persevere with stoicism via legerdemain? He has to promulgate the possibility of some discharge or other. What is the line from Goethe's *Faust* which so fascinated Sir Oswald Mosley that he had to introduce it? Right at the beginning, there was an action --- not a word. Note: that's the Christian gospel!

+

So Mezzanine Spratt decides on a course of definite enquiry. He guns the car's engine, presses his foot down on the accelerator, feeds it petrol and causes his vehicle to lurch forward in the rain. SLOSH! Wouldn't it be better to drive on and find a comfortable bed & breakfast? There'll be no dreaming on those pillows, then...

XII

Tanith Carpentier: "Do you see me – oppressed one of another existence? For I constantly stride towards a column of naked basalt; itself tempted over to a semblance of sequin. But still, it otherwise lists forwards and in every which way. Truly, a sap-swirl shows up aught amid a mist's declension, and many of my colleagues gather now somewhere in the darkness, well off to the west. Or might it amount to a leftist species, politically speaking? Anyway, the circumstances of this *Zeitgeist* have turned over on themselves. Didn't Julius Evola – the author of *Revolt Against the Modern World* – speak of a 'war of position' like in a Vesuvian chess match? Yess-s-s, since this gargoyle lolls over the side of your cranium in a dragon's get-up… it is waiting to still its distemper. Its refusal looks like a dinosaur, a brontosaurus or a pterodactyl, who waxes turquoise in its colour or delusion, and it waits to foment some ichor from its mouth. No matter how divine… while various magicians, dressed in orange loin-clouts, conjure up clouds on a large dais. They billow like a fortuitous haze or fug. Still, up above these rafters we detect elongated skeletons; each one of them carved in order to facilitate a goal. Whilst simultaneously – or at the behest of fountain-heads and pits – a shoal of dreams rips into prominence!

+

Certainly, a mystagogic presence lasts for a moment… and, like a moth liberated from its chrysalis, it lives for one day only. Surely, you know what's coming up from underground (?); well, it actually originates from the ether. It circles around – firing on all cylinders – with its teeth chuntering amid flaring gas or forgotten days. Great molars, whether curved or stretched, reach out to bite you: and they are part of a kaleidoscope or its revolving masks. Each one of them is aflame. In terms of nought to sixty seconds, though, these orbs gaze on distractedly or with a crystalline issue. Let's face it: they break out of flesh beyond its bone; they also harbour some essentially German art! These can be either Gothic or expressionist, as interpreted by Marcel Brion. Yet sincerely, these cripples rip forwards around a dwarf's head; if only to stretch around some vertebrae or its structures. All of it came to be submitted to a task, my lords, or it's rolled up into one nightmare. Assuredly – their hands reach out to you, themselves hooked onto nameless claws, and burning into one's skin (roundabouts). Do you notice it? Since each vessel of *kaos* was all aglow; at once ripping into dexterity's daybreak. Or –

rather alternatively – does it refuse to break free? Were such creatures – when gathered around the typewriter – an example of Nietzsche's *dawn*? Might they be salient and reduced unicorns, sabre-toothed monsters, demon spore, mugwumps, enlarged insects, fresh-faced louts and so much more? They can be described as a Comus Rout – one that pertains to John Milton's masque, for example. It (superintending all of this) is set to music by Henry Lawes.

+

Again, a great head whirled around Mezzanine or Tanith with an elongated snout. It proves to be basically blinded by ice or snow, and it laughed maniacally through lace-net curtains. Don't you remember Tanith's status as a Carthaginian moon goddess? But, in our pursuit's reality, it apes an intimation of Bedlam which reaches out for one. Furthermore, this gigantic jaw sprawls over in a lop-sided manner. 'HA! HA! HA! HA! HA! HA! HA! HA! HA! HA! HA! HA! HA! HA! HA!', it roared."

XIII

Meanwhile, we note with approval that Mezzanine Spratt has started his car moving again. Didn't it find a location beyond the grave? (Even we don't take notice of its absence, you see). Nonetheless, his red convertible veers onto the road and it belted off at a steady pace. Mezzanine drove on through the night with rain falling around his vehicle --- these happened to be great "swooshes" of water. Yes… a fine forest, almost like a wooded glade in Algernon Blackwood's work, lay around his head-lights in the night-time. Still, he pressed on into silence's envelope or outermost coin. Was there a mountain-side yonder (?); one which came limned in a pearlescent haze. It marvelled at its own blue – such proved to be the case. When suddenly Mezzanine Spratt surmounts a cross-roads… it has two signs, equidistant from each other, and on either side of a track within a forest. Does this vision come up before you now? Further to our point, two sigils stood in a masterful or heavy way. They existed adjacent to one another (*per se*) or within a hemicycle of the damned. Both seemed to be out of place; being vaguely magical, totemic, colophon gesturing, talismanic or whatever else. One road's direction is Bhagwan; the other indicates Maeohild. Truly, it notates a fork in the road, but whichever path down this tarot should one take? Mezzanine considers for a moment – now mentally alert – and he slowly moves his car down the duct marked Bhagwan. How was he to know whether one partiality spoke of Kali; the thugee's great goddess: while the other signalled an anglo-saxon heroine who virtually died of love? Aren't all novels really romances in disguise? For we're speaking of Bhowani, Bhadwan, Chamunda and Kali; or a thousand other evils. All of these betoken a recession in one's spirits…

XVI

Biff and Boff: "We know the answer, brethren! But we're not to tell it yet… because our tale hasn't reached its despoliation or climax. Still and all – within a tabernacle or its phantasy – one of Mezzanine Spratt's incarnations stood next to a roughly hewn sculpture. On closer inspection, then, it recalls one of those efforts by a modern master like Rodin. It stands on a plinth or minus a lugubrious *mien*; and it seems to be craggy, ill-absorbed, stratified, even archaic in its primitivism. Isn't 'it' splendid? Such an effort denies abstraction, but it looks to 'free' up this figure with a labile intensity. Won't you look at our offering? Since it reconnects *avec* Tanith's head only in passing… even to the extent where the mouth occasionally drops open: primarily so as to reveal a currency or its nethermost exchange. The sound when the mouth droops down is 'BBBOOOIING!' (…) despite the fact that no coin's left in this orifice *per se*. Behind Mezzanine – who curses at this prospect – comes the mute and silent figure of Biff. He wears an orange cowl. Whereas Spratt --- who's been caught in the head-lights like a rabbit --- sports Edwardian pyjamas.

+

Nor can one lose sight of Tanith Carpentier's severed head. Might it have been decapitated by Boff (?); when using one of those devices Doctor Guillotine made famous during the French Revolution. Besides all this, her skull's been picked up by one side; at once executed in purple or in such a way that can spit fire from green irises. In point of fact, her skinned orb floats up through swirling depths of red and brown… the like of which may be disturbed by advent's bell. But what did she have wedged between her teeth (my votary) other than a scarab beetle? An insect that'd crawled there in one's imagination; primarily in order to lance the boil of its mischance. For haven't you heard of every beetle drawing its sting? Of what, perchance (?); why, it's merely the unconscious…"

XV

Mezzanine kept on driving with his gloved hands fastened heavily to the wheel. What makes a man take one course of action rather than another? Sincerely, it has to do with the way the Norns have arranged things for you. Some call it karma or Fate. Whereas Mezzanine proceeded to drive on and he seems oblivious to crime or hazard, as he manoeuvred the round car under a thunder-storm. A burst of lightning lit up one's foreground – it proves to be attendant on a neglected view. And basically, it revolves around a disc of awe. Nor can we alleviate such a task! Great gaunt trees – of a sort which grew in this vicinity – sprouted out and upwards… All of them swayed diffidently on violent stalks! Never mind: the serrated edge of this rain swept all before it, and it keened or teamed to some prospect, but it was also leavened by a purchase on Odin's fury. He had never heard of Hurricane Katrina which plagued New Orleans so… Yet Mezzanine knew (somewhat dimly) that all 'progressive' notions fall sheer before Nature's majesty. No-one can choose their race, ethnicity, eugenic capacity, disabled absence, non-semitism, class strand, sexuality, intellect, beauty or lack of such. In these circumstances, environmentalism or social causation is catalepsy's lozenge. It subsists within a biological filter, quite evidently. For 'cultural studies' only replaces natural law with a new definition of the same. Whereupon marxism, in the form of Lenin's *Materialism and Empirico-criticism* or E.P. Thompson's *The New Reasoner*, stands refuted by a single example of one of Zeus' fiery bolts. Wasn't the Grecian all-father a master of our living lightning?

+

By some token of estrangement, therefore, Mezzanine became aware of lights among the trees. Surely a hamlet reared up amid this sward; itself nearly washed clean by oblivion's enemy? He decided to drive towards it.

XVI

She had seen him break free from the car or its screen, and this was primarily in order to seek shelter at an oubliette's portal. Might its outermost limit prove unfitted; primarily recalling that the vehicle which conveyed him was burnt sienna (even haemoglobin) in colour? On he ran across this shower and its spume. Yet, even as these diagonal sheets of wet speared him, he wondered about this village's deadness… that is: its parched, dry or brittle quality. Were any persons about? A brackish incense or smoke lurched from a neighbouring chimney… For, in the silence of *Saturn's Children*, there lies an implicit acceptance of chaos. Truly, he felt alone.

+

At the forefront of his mind – or in Spratt's conscious recollection – one gobbet fills the in-tray. In its tell-tale wonder, though, it has to do with asking directions to a filling station; at least prior to locating one highway in particular… All of which occurs due to a process of reverse mesmerism. But truthfully, another filter in his cranium leads this chariot forwards. She sensed it also; especially when pursuant to a gathering in her cave: one that's superintended by a one-eyed Cyclops.

Tanith Carpentier stands with a cottage door open beside her. "I facilitate the coming embrace of your uncertainty!", she declared.

"Friend, future lover and husband... listen to me. You were once my slave – in that the listless object of your abandoned eyes led you to me. Not a sense of contingency, no, but a beguiling magnetism from Robert Graves' *The White Goddess* brought you here. Quickly – at once fix the complexity of these dreams to my poniard; a dagger that's strapped next to my naked thigh by a thread of gold. It happens to be transparent in its lucidity. Do you detect its faintness – now – when akin to the bronzed leg pulsating 'neath it?"

Mezzanine Spratt: "Who are you?"

Tanith Carpentier: "May well you stare – stranger – at my breath-taking beauty. Let's consider it to be an example of Cleopatra's knowing innocence... Most especially, when it takes place with an Egyptian 'dome' of hair; the latter amber to its lit nectar... plus blue-lips which were aflame with passion, and fluorescent eye-shadow smeared around Basilisk reaches. Can you detect their Ophidian lusts? Doesn't the White Rastafarian hair-do – when pleated in its peroxide magnificence – recall *Lulu*? You remember her Stygian vaultedness? For she was the main character (or a nymphomaniac lodestar) in Alban Berg's opera. But – to reverse a spell or some feminine fatigue – my armour bears upon it a trace of Macha; i.e., the female crone in Celtic mythology. And all of this occurs at a time when she's revered next to a raven's tracery!"

Mezzanine Spratt: "Where are we?"

Tanith Carpentier: "Do these dreams fail to instruct those frontal lobes in Gray's *Anatomy* (?) – according to which your physical co-ordinates are traced. Wayward man, you have been drawn towards a concealed magnet under chlorinated paper, in relation to that 'O' level experiment in physics. Wherein Farraday's postulates were signed off for, as regards ferrous filings and their electro-magnetism.

+

Loving one, my game of snakes and ladders has led you to a sorcerer's village. Here magic reigns without any brook, stint or surcease. It comes to be altogether untrammelled. Perhaps it would do you good to think of yourself as a character trapped inside Dennis Wheatley's semiotic, or in a novel like *The Satanist*... for example. How can one of Pirandello's six gain egress to this hamlet, you ask? Why, it may often come about on wild and stormy nights – to quote Bulwer Lytton out of context. It's only then that strangers or outsiders will find the portal to a forbidden cosmogony. Do you navigate around the metaphor of a green door made of wood (?), an entrance whose substance conceals a magic garden behind a wall. It encloses it completely. (Whether one masters 'it' in fictions as diverse as those of Rosamund Lehmann or Arthur Machen, depending...) Remember: once you've gained entry by dint of free will, our multiple version of a three-headed Cerberus won't let you out! Too late; they have detected your presence. Like me, Mezzanine love, you entered on a billowing even-song --- only to never be allowed out by them."

Mezzanine Spratt: "Who are *they*?"

Tanith Carpentier: "The Magicians..."

XVII

Biff and Boff, dressed in purple vestments, appear behind them. A motley collection of ill-assorted mountebanks follow on – rather like a choked-off sea. All of these wear close-fitting masks about their features, reminiscent of the painter Ensor, and under their magenta hoods.

Biff and Boff are scarcely able to conceal a sadistic munificence. "Hark, a delinquent aberration has appeared amongst us from without. Are you aware – daughter of us all – that the circle had been transgressed by one whose hands and mouth have known contamination by unhallowed meats? Might he prove to be porcine; in terms readily available concerning a novel known as *The Pork Butcher*? No matter: you may not speak... at least with the leaden zipper we have placed over your lips. *Avaunt thee* – false Beelzebub – your lineaments manifest themselves through wrath's aptitude. Listen (turning to their male captive) you have nowhere to go but down adjacent to this loam.

+

HA! HA! HA! HA! HA! HA! HA! HA HA! HA! Let us reminisce about the following imbroglio... Mightn't it reconnect with a scene where shaven-headed troopers stand muster? They all sit in serried rows, ranks or phalanxes. Do you comprehend it? Whereupon they manoeuvre a three-pronged utensil about their person. It busily travels above a cube of gruel; if only to descend on it with a thud or crunch. Likewise, the look on these youths' faces remains serene or placid, and they're possibly untroubled before the day's ordeals. Certainly, these ephebes recall a squad of marines or commandos rather than a bohemian dispensation... redolent of so many *jeunesse doree*. On closer inspection, though, one of them delineates Mezzanine Spratt's features – albeit in silhouette. They are gaunt, yet discernibly adolescent. Suddenly a voice cracks forth: 'Desist from such consumption... Don't eat it, Spratt! Each cuboid is rancid beyond any prospect of salience. It contains some brain-drain chemical; the latter destined to chill those factors within.' But who advances towards such a fulsome warning? Why, it happens to be a middle-aged version of Biff; a creature who's merely leavened to its course and flying abroad on a sort of electronic bath-chair. A seating arrangement which seems to be accompanied with much gadgetry. He also appears invisible to those youthful myrmidons gathered roundabouts. They carry on munching regardless, even though our phantom still continues to speak. 'You'll need all of your faculties, my boy. Remember: you must clear up the mind and control it... it belongs to you.' On closer inspection, however, it becomes noticeable that half of Biff's face is covered in blue... with some sort of spherical emblem emblazoned across it. He points at Mezzanine with a long arching finger. Moreover, a gauntlet encloses its outermost development (betimes). Didn't his mother ever tell him it's rude to point? To which Spratt responds by shouting: 'Shut up! By Ymir, silence is golden in terms of its plenitude.' Even though – in response to this – his erstwhile cohort sees nothing at all. Everything remains invisible to them (as a consequence) and they look about their number in perplexity. 'There he goes again', says one. 'Hasn't he developed a fetish for ranting against empty air? Doesn't he discern whether one's ether comes chock full with demons – like in a Hieronymous Bosch painting?' Mezzanine responds without really answering. He stares onwards rather moodily. Perhaps, in a manner put forward by Colin Forbes in *The Endless Game*, he realises that quietness waxes infinitely precious. Ask for John Cage's endorsement here… But, even at a tender age, Spratt felt himself to be unburdened by a gadfly voice."

XVIII

Tanith Carpentier <<<with a voice echoing inside her suitor's mind>>>: "Hold on now, lover. They are coming for you across Breugel's morose wasteland, but there is no need to fear. Since courage will fasten to its regard abreast of a barren acreage of values. Moreover, do you remember the activism of a dream? Wherein one particular recruit was led towards a punishment squad, itself situated to the side of a sandy plain, and adjacent to various modernist structures reminiscent of Mies van der Rohe. Do you bring back Ayn Rand's *The Fountainhead* to memory, as seen through a grisaille's angularity? No matter, my eye-candy of choice… For such xylography depicts a phalanx of shaven-headed youths – all of them in serried rows and about to administer discipline. It could involve 'running the gauntlet' at a public school; after the fashion of an antique custom at Rugby like quad flogging, for example. Yet here, the young troopers array themselves around a miscreant whom they're eager to strike. Each one of them draws back a reflex's baton – albeit when ready to run through one of their number who hasn't made the grade. 'We'll tighten you up, weakling', suggests one of them with a snide smirk. Another remarks: 'let's rifle him out with a halbert… or a combined spear and its battle-axe.' 'Enough talk', wheedles another, 'I'm anxious to beat upon such meat.' In response to this remark or tasking, a younger version of Mezzanine utters the following words: 'You boneless larvae, I despise you all! Go on, take your kicks, you wretches or spawn. Do your worst…' 'AAAAAGGGHHH!', they cry in unison. 'Prevail upon him not to pass out of your mission, at least in relation to a posting next to oblivion. Yes sir…' 'Make way, remove your shoulder from the bladed bone. I want to crack those legs, primarily so as to execute the marrow within. Aha! Let's look at such a ventriloquist's spiralling orb. Have I fixed him to the work bench by placing a pin via a rare beetle, thereby?'"

Simultaneously though, doesn't this intone an earlier performance of Punch and Judy? A scenario or playlet (it is) where Punch's figurine emerges from behind a purple cloak. May Sir Harrison Birtwhistle's atonality accord with our swazzler's psychic attributes? Only Mezzanine stands continuously on this shingle or outside the booth – never mind its sound. For there were no other children to respond to the 'blood and thunder' of such a *Grand Guignol*. Truly, the child within us often requires violent emotions… nearly all of them set off against a moral code of absolutes. Yet not even metaphysical objectivism can compete with a wall of dolls; each one of these laid out photographically by Waldo Lanchester. Do we really fail to respond to their grinning teeth, revolving eyes, sinister mien and *papier-mâché* heads? This is never mind the pomegranates of such a bestiary which were lost behind an ovoid touch – necessarily, of so many hachures."

XIX

Yet these turquoise-clad mages have elemental tones at their command, such as a flickering flame or an Indian rope-trick. "Up lasso", they proclaim to an inanimate object... "Go to the outsider, bind him hand and foot – or fast and loose!"

Mezzanine Spratt: "What is this?"

Biff and Boff: "It remains nought but our rendition of a full metal jacket. Have you yet to recognise the labyrinthine quality of your dreams? Within which you might savour a miasma's displacement; at once delivered headless or redolent of Punch's gibbet – plus a cranium in a box. Doesn't such a Headman indicate a sense of panic? Necessarily, since water and fire are both alchemical symbols of a 'heretic' world! Furthermore, any adventure must take note of your relative light-headedness... Given that Tanith Carpentier walked away from Mezzanine, who was held captive in a bath, with various hippogriffs appointed on every corner. She stalked on amidst a velvet green (most definitely), *avec* the latter twisting and turning adjacent to illumined piles... all of them Gothic to this last. They rose up out of a tessellated floor; together with the ghoulish exhibition of many victims lassoed above. Might these cadavers codify one of those 'plastinates' by the anatomist, Professor Gunter von Hagens? Still, a pink embrasure filled this scene's monstrous or composite body... given those blue tiles, in a perfect symmetry, that provide a mesmerism over one's floor-sheen. In its arithmetic – then – this parquet harks back to a mosaic or (alternatively) a *lapis* drawn from Islamic art. Also, behind her hyacinth a dioxaxine purple swept away; the former showing Biff or myself in silhouette. While those reptilian fancies – when borne aloft by their mystification – began to shower Mezzanine with a sulphuric indent. He lay, for his part, chained to the inside of a cylindrical vessel... within which such toads are free to vomit their fancy!

+

Do they reinterpret those creatures in Hieronymous Bosch's painting, *The Temptation of Saint Anthony*? For here, they besport themselves within the alabaster of a new roof or its tiles.

Yet – on occasion – a snout-faced imp who's dressed in black, while being porcine, and with a mandolin or flute… why, he has occasion to cross a threshold between life and death. Isn't that the case? *L'homme propose et Dieu dispose…* now what about the owl which happens to be perched on his scalp? Because all such polycephalous spectres must come to a point where they resemble this. Again, each figure is maimed or becalmed in its quietude – when possibly adjacent to a machine that looks on with indifference or alters its trajectory of sepulchral gloom. Finally, why does a virginal figurine o'erstraddle the saint (?) while proffering a dish of Holy Water. In comparison to which – various owls make hay with an arrested purity (sic) and this occurs before some scales of oneiric defeat. Yes… these mediums have sought to lift a veil on the next life; if only to cast a semblance upon a twilight; a chiaroscuro. Do you detect its import? Since this tenuity of the perverse renders itself aloof in different manikins; themselves shrunken or denoting dwarves. All in all, they mushroom out as the Grotesques of illuminated manuscripts… the like of it merely bewildering a margin. Are these jottings really the incunabula of a bygone age?"

XX

Mezzanine Spratt: "My body or physiog(.) has been concocted by a rope – the levitation of which surrounds my curlew. It holds me bitterly to its entreaty's shaft (betimes). Are we reminded of one of John Cowper Powys' early fictions? These mages think that they've bound me hand and foot… but Tanith stands beside me. She leans against my blue-garbed body, so that the weight of her hand conceals something. It writhes adjacent to her scarlet dress."

Meanwhile, the purple-clad magicians gather in a hemicycle around their two 'victims'. A strange hum seems to come up from their serried mouths. For a brief moment it brings to mind a Greek chorus – whether in terms of its strophe or antistrophe, and always pursuant to a tragedy. (Whether Peter Jones teaches us the language or not). Doesn't such an assemblage – when gathered together from two and a half millennia ago – consist of old men in masks? Moreover, each and every one of them fails to put forward a different view… given that *Lex talionis* indicates a law of retribution.

Biff and Boff are referring to their stuffed arm-pits: "Look forwards to this, the two of you! Since to one side of the demon which haunts Saint Anthony, and that seems accustomed to a leftwards drift, a rival figurine or Old Father Time emerges. It is a cripple who's locked into self-trespass, but otherwise carries a burden of servitude. He shuffles onwards with one make-belief before his game – almost as if he can play a musical instrument. Could it be a harp or an Iberian guitar in the hands of one skilled to use it – like John Williams, perchance? Never mind: *quod* the aspect adopted by these anthropomorphic forms must know their own minds. Yet, irrespective of such a dint, our tapered wraiths maximise their circumference or leave nought to chance. Here flits half an owl – when nearly filleted to some smoke – and glowering before the tempera of a new engagement. It also rescues its plinth; in a manner which makes a mockery of a game of chance proceeding on a table that's circular in its hewn gambit. Various biomorphic tents whisk about --- some part vegetal --- while others track a beetle's thorax to its lair. Don't we register this (?); even in the dream with which this narrative has been plagued hitherto. Because once the girl, Tanith, wanders off with her accompanying magicians… they can cut off her head using a mock-guillotine! It was originally concealed behind a hillock that's essentially russet in hue. Whilst a homunculus or *invunche* drained out the gore from her severed neck into a porcelain bowl. Mightn't it have been manufactured from spode china; the latter at once rare over its reflexes on the distaff side? Even so: she remains alive --- in spite of all."

Tanith speaks herself now; and her irises are brightly lit up so as to fill the available sockets. No astigmatism really fails to communicate a story here (therefore).

Tanith Carpentier: "One's head-chicken sprouts off or aft, and you're even free to make a wish. For where has all of this blue-blood come from – like in the first stages of an infant's birth? Ugh! You see, yonder pot contains those daemonic innards which belaboured one's insides… at least before relief. What purpose do one's intestines have when confronted by the gutting knife, eh? It's definitely a poniard too far, one feels. Yes, my spirituality makes free to float like a bird who's unburdened by the spirit. But truly, any writhing impermanence must mark its time… for my aspic certainty (when forlorn of issue) finds its wonder sacrificed before such a miracle. My head was off, you know, and bouncing like a ball with its green eyes distended. Most particularly – when the basic colour of a scalp remains pearlescent and nacreous, and it rode its luck if surrounded by a rose penumbra. All I could manage by way of a shout remained: 'UGGHH…glug-glug-glug!' Not to worry, though: since one's rootedness to the ground has to involve an absence of legs. Perhaps now, my decapitated rind can be picked up by Biff who moves next to a stalk – or a root – of the brightest yellow."

Mezzanine Spratt finds himself pursuant to an internal swazzle. "You must never forget the advanced reproach of 'Saint Anthony's temptation', however! A scenario wherein the saint wears a grey cowl next to his affected grace; irrespective of any surrounding loucheness. Do you realise the solace or redemption now afoot? For one permitted larceny remains within a sow's recognition or ken, and at least in terms of a *grey eminence* that occasionally lists towards black. He or 'it' approaches Saint Anthony sideways-on; and yet such a will-o'-the-wisp comes to be undefeated by silence. Do you recall its similarity to a copper-head… that is: the most poisonous snake on the north american mainland? Or alternatively, this summons up from the depths a pulp-fiction character who was unlicensed by any metallic conduction. May it comprehend a magic camera's momentum, thereafter? Because this sloth creature – or necessary gut-wrench – loomed up mercurially from the side. Whereas his movements were ungainly and stiff; at once re-interpreting a hippy on over-drive or the shambling gait of a beatnik. Could this possibly register the mincing pass of one of Jack Kerouac's desolation angels? None of which ever chooses to mind the empty call of Thomas Pynchon's 'Lot 49' or Kathy Acker's Algiers – the latter Sapphically smeared. Again, it slid into position with a toxic banjo to hand, and do we detect an old-fashioned pistol in its belt or buttress? Let's see now: the pig-man zig-zagged on towards our Church Father or his Church of the Creator; with black satin then accompanying any impediment to *Facial Justice*. Wasn't that an anti-socialist novel by L.P. Hartley, and didn't such a troubadour make way for an unlikely exorcism?" (Note: the Church of the Creator is a supremacist sect founded by Ben Klassen).

XXI

Our black magicians – when garbed in a grey lotus' diet – stood around the fire-storm of their own manufacture. Tanith's head was off or distracted now, and her golden eyes glinted dully in the dust. Isn't this a roseate distillation coming up for fresh air (?); and always existing amid a watery grave-time. Still, the liquids of such an impermanence have a brown streak shot through their hybrid essence. Might it embody an ochre tincture – while captured to its available loss – and swirling with opaque depths mushrooming at its centre? Anyway, in comparison to this, Tanith's bifurcated globule found itself supported in these shadows… Whilst her eyes let loose a delicate stream by way of a rivulet; at least in terms of some ready salted tears. In passing an eldritch compass, then, didn't Iris Murdoch write an early fable called *A Severed Head*?

+

Carpentier's skull embodies a delicate brushstroke at this point, with an earthy sediment roundabout it. Were these orbs close to such a feasting; at least in comparison to the tousled lushness of her hair. Does one detect its unforgiving quality? Whereupon her arms hook up blankly in a stupor, so as to master the adamantine quality of those glass-eyes. Much of which means that an M.R. James story comes into play: (i.e., a variant on Harrison Birtwhistle's chamber opera *Punch and Judy*, with a libretto and vocal score by Stephen Pruslin). Nonetheless, the sluice-gates behind those doll's-eyes make ready for action, primarily so as to carom a blue-green marble into each socket. Irrespective of this – a beetle's antennae are seen to emerge out of her mouth; the former after a black opal's impress. May such an insect's shadow mount a tattoo on the tongue, basically so as to summon up woad's constancy? Look at this: a *Coleoptera* whose upper wings have been converted into cases ... why, it emerges from her laughing-stick's taste. It seems redundant before the flying creature's mandibles. For every beetle draws a sting – don't you know? (In any event, a BBC repeat like this harks back to Nietzsche's 'The Endless Return').

XXII

Tanith Carpentier: "I have a knife to hand which is hidden within the folds of my cloak... It happens to be next to your sapphire-coloured mack. (She was addressing Mezzanine Spratt at the time and in a low whisper). For, like a maiden of the church who comforts Saint Anthony, I leant across a silent salvo that's undaunted over its own closure (primarily). My dress, in such circumstances, trammels the list of a delicate pink – especially when it's taken together with the brilliantly white shawl around my head. Don't I offer sweet-meats – or even a compendium of water – in terms of a God in the Bowl?"

Biff and Boff were surrounded by lesser grand masters at this time. "Unsurprisingly, we are ahead of you, my dear, and at the discretion of our thinking. Because the presence of the daemonic is little more than a tad-pole to our entreaty! Given this, one crippled lutanist approaches a red hearth amidst twilight. Mightn't he be playing his forlorn stick oblivious of all else (?), and when accompanied by a carnival dog: a mutt which wears a wine-hood about its cheeks. Do you retain a necessary regard for these facts? Most particularly – when we consider that those reptiles which do so, Tanith, move eastwards from the west to the accompaniment of ochre. It settles, this latter gradient, upon a chocolate dispensation --- that is, a chiaroscuro which was shot through with dissembling fire that's akin to reddish egg tempera. But still, these hog-heads or heresiarchs move closer to Saint Anthony – all the time composing that lute music which spoke of an alchemical 'bridal chamber'. Yess-ss-ss."

Tanith Carpentier: "Tell me, my coven of warlocks, what befell my head in another dimension – particularly when it had been severed from its trunk?"

Those male witches who are gathered in conclave merely sneer in reply: "Why don't you use your imagination, girl?"

For what fate opens up – while pursuant to this Death's-head – can only be the following volute… in which, *mutatis mutandis*, the knife, spear, arrow, sword and axe all make an appearance. They are assorted emblems of alchemical fire and each helps to feed its furnace's mysteries. Do us a favour, will you? This occurs by virtue of the fact that your head has swivelled free from its corse, if only to manoeuvre out beyond any night-time borders. Are you really brave enough to see? Further: your plastinate's face found itself linked to a steel balustrade – one which is contained, as it was, within a plexiglass cage. Can an observer possibly remember the alternative character of scientific romance known as Doctor Sun? Never mind: her pate or scalp whips around in a whirligig; and it caroms like a billiard or snooker ball with a sigil upon its tongue that indicates a beetle's impress. At the same time, though, any attempt to grasp her head-tennis causes it to rear up like a careering fun-fair device. She can even travel across the floor – especially if it happens to be shiny and translucent in texture. Isn't it reminiscent of sand after it has undergone nuclear fission? Yes indeed, if we wish to speak radioactively… (Even though this mute truckle-bed can embody one of those Boer War cripples, drawn by Grosz and L.S. Lowry, and made use of by Brecht). Finally, Tanith's decapitation veers off with a sudden *élan*; if only for its cage to become clamped to a rocket's boosters. It then soars into outer space and follows the elliptical passage of such a projectile. Thereafter, and rather like one of NASA's shuttles, it is blown to smithereens in the outermost ether."

XXIII

Tanith Carpentier: "Quickly beloved, your hands are free thanks to the temporary insistence of my knife. Let us run for your car which exists at the heart of the square in this hamlet… a factor that's just like the village of Port Meirion in Patrick McGoohan's *The Prisoner*. Nothing will be able to stop us now; irrespective of those two ghoulish magicians who stand guard next to your convertible. Move my trampoline and make haste – we've got to get out of this place (to use an old Blue Oyster cult song); and we must cross the threshold from one reality into another one."

Mezzanine Spratt: "Now that I've found you, I'm not going without you."

Tanith Carpentier: "Darling, you help to grant me a courage comparable to your own. With you beside me, all last vestiges of fear are stripped from me!"

The mages Biff and Boff were now possibly screaming for the last time: "STOP… don't pass forward towards this tunnel of flame. We command you!" <<<A momentum which subsists slightly afore her rush to the automobile; an escape that's aided and abetted by Mezzanine.>>>

++

OPERATION FAST-FORWARD: *if we were to use the future perfect…*

Biff and Boff: “Move away from his circumference, Tanith, lest you wish to undergo exquisite pain – such as a salutary beheading! Don’t doubt over whether it will be artistically accomplished, sweetie. For by any other commando issue, though, Up Flame… go to them and summon their obedience to our power. If we might invert Aleister Crowley’s diction, hate shall be the whole of the law! Again Waves – prevent the completion of their egress and lock them out (then) within the dancing juniper of your tidal spume.”

Irrespective of any of this, however, our two outlaws have reached the car; if only to see it submerged by a cascading wavelet. Still, do they manage to make it out of the village – albeit with water lapping around their stagecoach on every side? The vehicle’s engine roars into life and they create some necessary tracks as a consequence.

XXIV=XXVII

Mezzanine woke up a while later in his cabin. He had had the temerity to fall asleep in his work’s craft throughout. A liquid wetness has entered the cab from somewhere – yet he remains alone and somewhat bereft. Let’s consider the following analogy: might this be an example of English heroic legend or folk-tale, as narrated by Kathleen Herbert? Anyway, may this entire imbroglio have been a dream (?); or some sort of phantasm of waking consciousness? Mezzanine Spratt rubbed his chin for a moment – he couldn’t make his mind up between the two alternatives. But Tanith, beloved Tanith, with the red skin, blonde hair, large bust and blue-and-white bikini… surely she was real? Maybe, he mused aloud to himself. Yet if she were chimerical – why did she leave such a definite impression? He wound the window down for an instant in order to access some fresh air. Reluctantly he was forced to gun the engine, bank the roadster up and career off. After a wee while he came to a crossroads which loomed up around a curve or bend, and with two signs facing in opposite directions. It's all happening as before, he thought... Dimly, he remembered that one side gave out the clarion known as Bhagwan; while the other one called after a lost maiden named Maeohild. It rather absently flitted across his mind whether their respective designs embody a cool painting – with the affectation of collage – by Juan Gris. Moreover, the rain continues to pour down in straight sheets around his automobile (betimes). Whilst his windscreen wipers roared and slapped on nine to the dozen. What to do now? Bizarrely, his sub-conscious had told him whatever the wooden balustrades would say before he spied them... Most fantastical – and rather like Hieronymous Bosch's celebration of St. Anthony's ordeal, he conspired to think. Wasn't he serenaded by a sense of creeping or postlapsarian life, even in death? Possibly... he also registered that the whole caboodle seemed to be a psychotic fancy – yet the girl's presence still appealed to him. Couldn't she be a moral species of *erotica* (?), or even the exact opposite to Rouault's delineation of fury in paint? Certainly, my man... Maybe it all took place and the sorcerers made him relive it – rather filmically – as a form of post-structural *doxa*? After which intervention (though) it would be time enough to take the tamer route down Maeohild way... yes, the case happens to be closed at this juncture. THEN IT SUDDENLY HITS HIM WITH THE FORCE OF A REVELATION. 'Tanith's in Bhagwan. She's reliant on me. I have to rescue her. Darling, I won't fail you!' He knew it all at a definite point. For one's colours – within the vestibule of a cab – were basically red and black now. Mezzanine Spratt's life has been forever altered (you see), and, in masculine terms, courage had become the only possible morality.

FINIS

DID3602143
L - #0210 - 090623 - C0 - 229/152/10 - PB - DID3602143